THE ET

From Nu's throat rose t
people – a cry that brought a
their feet trembling in fear or in rage. Victoria
watched the two men who battled for her. She saw the handsome black head of the savage bend lower towards the throat of his foe, saw the strong jaws rend and tear the soft flesh, saw her ferocious mate shake the man as a terrier shakes a rat, and her heart swelled in fierce primitive pride.

No longer did Victoria Custer exist. It was Nat-ul, daughter of Tha, Nat-ul of the tribe of Nu that dwelt beyond the Barren Cliffs and beside the Restless Sea, who threw her arms about her lord and master's neck. For a time she had been carried back a hundred thousand years to the childhood of the human race – she had not known for those brief instants Victoria Custer, or the twentieth century, or its civilisation, for they were yet a thousand centuries in the future.

Also by Edgar Rice Burroughs

AT THE EARTH'S CORE
PELLUCIDAR
TANAR OF PELLUCIDAR
BACK TO THE STONE AGE
LAND OF TERROR
SAVAGE PELLUCIDAR

THE LAND THAT TIME FORGOT
THE PEOPLE THAT TIME FORGOT
OUT OF TIME'S ABYSS

THE MOON MAID
THE MOON MEN

BEYOND THE FARTHEST STAR
THE MONSTER MEN
THE LAND OF HIDDEN MEN

Edgar Rice Burroughs

THE ETERNAL SAVAGE

TANDEM

A TANDEM BOOK
published by
WYNDHAM PUBLICATIONS

A Tandem Book
published in 1976
by Wyndham Publications Ltd
A Howard & Wyndham Company
123 King Street, London W6 9JG

Originally published in the United States under the title
The Eternal Lover

Made and printed in Great Britain by
Cox & Wyman Ltd, London, Reading and Fakenham

ISBN 0426 17857 2

PART ONE

CHAPTER ONE

NU OF THE NIOCENE

Nu, the son of Nu, his mighty muscles rolling beneath his smooth bronzed skin, moved silently through the jungle primeval. His handsome head with its shock of black hair, roughly cropped between sharpened stones, was high held, the delicate nostrils questioning each vagrant breeze for word of Oo, hunter of men.

Now his trained senses catch the familiar odor of Ta, the great woolly rhinoceros, directly in his path, but Nu, the son of Nu, does not hunt Ta this day. Does not the hide of Ta's brother already hang before the entrance of Nu's cave? No, today Nu hunts the gigantic cat, the fierce saber-toothed tiger, Oo, for Nat-ul, wondrous daughter of old Tha, will mate with none but the mightiest of hunters.

Only so recently as the last darkness, as, beneath the great, equatorial moon, the two had walked hand in hand beside the restless sea she had made it quite plain to Nu, the son of Nu, that not even he, son of the chief of chiefs, could claim her unless there hung at the thong of his loin cloth the fangs of Oo.

'Nat-ul,' she had said to him, 'wishes her man to be greater than other men. She loves Nu now better than her very life, but if Love is to walk at her side during a long life Pride and Respect must walk with it.' Her slender hand reached up to stroke the young giant's black hair. 'I am very proud of my Nu even now,' she continued, 'for among all the young men of the tribe there is no greater hunter, or no mightier fighter than Nu, the son of Nu. Should you, single-handed, slay Oo before a grown man's beard has darkened your cheek there will be none greater in all the world than Nat-ul's mate, Nu, the son of Nu.'

The young man was still sensible to the sound of her soft voice and the caress of her gentle touch upon his brow. As these things had sent him speeding forth into the savage jungle in search of Oo while the day was still so young that the night-prowling beasts of prey were yet abroad, so they urged him forward deeper and deeper into the dark and trackless mazes of the tangled forest.

As he forged on the scent of Ta became stronger, until at last the huge, ungainly beast loomed large before Nu's eyes. He was standing in a little clearing, in deep, rank jungle grasses, and had he not been head on toward Nu he would not have seen him, since even his acute hearing was far too dull to apprehend the noiseless tread of the cave man, moving lightly up wind.

As the tiny, blood-shot eyes of the primordial beast discovered the man the great head went down, and Ta, ill natured and bellicose progenitor of the equally ill natured and bellicose rhino of the twentieth century, charged the lithe giant who had disturbed his antediluvian meditation.

The creature's great bulk and awkward, uncouth lines belied his speed, for he tore down upon Nu with all the swiftness of a thoroughbread and had not the brain and muscle of the troglodyte been fitted by heritage and training to the successful meeting of such emergencies there would be no tale to tell today of Nu of the Niocene.

But the young man was prepared, and turning he ran with the swiftness of a hare toward the nearest tree, a huge, arboraceous fern towering upon the verge of the little clearing. Like a cat the man ran up the perpendicular bole, his hands and feet seeming barely to touch the projecting knobs marking the remains of former fronds which converted the towering stem into an easy stairway for such as he.

About Nu's neck his stone-tipped spear hung by its rawhide thong down his back, while stone hatchet and stone knife dangled from his gee-string, giving him free use of his hands for climbing. You or I, having once gained the seeming safety of the lowest fronds of the great tree, fifty feet above the ground, might have heaved a great sigh of relief that we had thus easily escaped the hideous monster beneath; but not so Nu, who was wise to the ways of the creatures of his remote age.

Not one whit did he abate his speed as he neared the lowest branch, nor did he even waste a precious second in a downward glance at his enemy. What need, indeed? Did he not know precisely what Ta would do? Instead he swung, monkey-like, to the broad leaf, and though the chances he took would have paled the face of a brave man today they did not cause Nu even to hesitate, as he ran lightly and swiftly along the bending, swaying frond, leaping just at the right instant toward the bole of a nearby jungle giant.

Nor was he an instant too soon. The frond from which he had sprung had scarce whipped up from beneath his weight when Ta, with all the force and momentum of a runaway locomotive, struck the base of the tree head on. The jar of that terrific collision shook the earth, there was the sound of the splintering of wood, and the mighty tree toppled to the ground with a deafening crash.

Nu, from an adjoining tree, looked down and grinned. He was not hunting Ta that day, and so he sprang from tree to tree until he had passed around the clearing, and then, coming to the surface once more, continued his way toward the distant lava cliffs where Oo, the man hunter, made his grim lair.

From among the tangled creepers through which the man wormed his sinuous way ugly little eyes peered down upon him from beneath shaggy, beetling brows, and great fighting tusks were bared, as the hairy ones growled and threatened from above; but Nu paid not the slightest attention to the huge, ferocious creatures that menaced him upon every hand. From earliest childhood he had been accustomed to the jabberings and scoldings of the ape-people, and so he knew that if he went his way in peace, harming them not, they would offer him no harm. One of lesser experience might have attempted to drive them away with menacing spear, or well-aimed hatchet, and thus have drawn down upon him a half dozen or more ferocious bulls against which no single warrior, however doughty, might have lived long enough to count his antagonists.

Threatening and unfriendly as the apes seemed the cave man really looked upon them as friends and allies, since between them and his own people there existed a species of friendly alliance, due no doubt to the similarity of their form and structure. In that long gone age when the world was young and its broad bosom teemed with countless thousands of carnivorous beasts and reptiles, and other myriads blackened the bosoms of its inland seas, and filled its warm, moist air with the flutter of their mighty, bat-like wings, man's battle for survival stretched from sun to sun – there was no respite. His semiarboreal habits took him often into the domains of the great and lesser apes, and from this contact had arisen what might best be termed an armed truce, for they alone of all the other inhabitants of the earth had spoken languages, both meager it is true, yet sufficient to their primitive wants, and as both languages had been born of the same needs to deal with identical conditions there were many words and phrases identical to both. Thus the troglodyte and the primordial ape could converse when necessity demanded, and as Nu traversed their country he understood their grumbling and chattering merely as warnings to him against the performance of any overt act. Had danger lurked in his path the hairy ones would have warned him of that too, for of such was their service to man who in return often hunted the more remorseless of their enemies, driving them from the land of the anthropoids.

On and on went Nu occasionally questioning the hairy ones he encountered for word of Oo, and always the replies confirmed him in his belief that he should come upon the man eater before the sun crawled into its dark cave for the night.

And so he did. He had passed out of the heavier vegetation, and was ascending a gentle rise that terminated in low volcanic cliffs when there came down upon the breeze to his alert nostrils the strong scent of Oo. There was little or no cover now, other than the rank jungle grass that overgrew the slope, and an occasional lofty fern rearing its tufted pinnacle a hundred feet above the ground; but Nu was in no way desirous of cover. Cover that would protect him from the view of Oo would hide Oo from him. He was not afraid that the saber-toothed tiger would run away from him – that was not Oo's way – but he did not wish to come unexpectedly upon the animal in the thick grass.

He had approached to within a hundred yards of the cliffs now, and the scent of Oo had become as a stench in the sensitive nostrils of the cave man. Just ahead he could see the openings to several caves in the face of the rocky barrier, and in one of these he knew must lie the lair of his quarry.

Fifty yards from the cliff the grasses ceased except for scattered tufts that had found foothold among the broken rocks that strewed the ground, and as Nu emerged into this clear space he breathed a sigh of relief for during the past fifty yards a considerable portion of the way had been through a matted jungle that rose above his head. To have met Oo there would have spelled almost certain death for the cave man.

Now, as he bent his eyes toward the nearby cave mouths he discovered one before which was strewn such an array of gigantic bones that he needed no other evidence as to the identity of its occupant. Here, indeed, laired no lesser creature than the awesome Oo, the gigantic, saber-toothed tiger of antiquity. Even as Nu looked there came a low and ominous growl from the dark mouth of the foul cavern, and then in the blackness beyond the entrance Nu saw two flaming blotches of yellow glaring out upon him.

A moment later the mighty beast itself sauntered majestically into the sunlight. There it stood lashing its long tail from side to side, glaring with unblinking eyes straight at the rash man-thing who dared venture thus near its abode of death. The huge body, fully as large as that of a full grown bull, was beautifully marked with black stripes upon a vivid yellow ground, while the belly and breast were of the purest white.

As Nu advanced the great upper lip curled back revealing in all their terrible ferocity the eighteen inch curved fangs that armed either side of the upper jaw, and from the cavernous throat came a fearsome scream of rage that brought frightened silence upon the jungle for miles around.

The hunter loosened the stone knife at his gee-string and transferred it to his mouth where he held it firmly, ready for instant use, between his strong, white teeth. In his left hand he carried his stone-tipped spear, and in his right the heavy stone hatchet that was so effective both at a distance and at close range.

Oo is creeping upon him now. The grinning jaws drip saliva. The yellow-green eyes gleam bloodthirstily. Can it be possible that this fragile pygmy dreams of meeting in hand-to-hand combat the terror of a world, the scourge of the jungle, the hunter of men and of mammoths?

'For Nat-ul,' murmured Nu, for Oo was about to spring.

As the mighty hurtling mass of bone and muscle, claws and fangs, shot through the air toward him the man swung his tiny stone hatchet with all the power behind his giant muscles, timing its release so nicely that it caught Oo in mid leap squarely between the eyes with the terrific force of a powder sped projectile. Then Nu, cat-like as Oo himself, leaped agilely to one side as the huge bulk of the beast dashed, sprawling to the ground at the spot where the man had stood.

Scarce had the beast struck the earth than the cave man, knowing that his puny weapon could at best but momentarily stun the monster, drove his heavy spear deep into the glossy side just behind the giant shoulder.

Already Oo has regained his feet, roaring and screaming in pain and rage. The air vibrates and the earth trembles to his hideous shrieks. For miles around the savage denizens of the savage jungle bristle in terror, slinking further into the depths of their dank and gloomy haunts, casting the while affrighted glances rearward in the direction of that awesome sound.

With gaping jaws and wide spread talons the tiger lunges toward its rash tormentor who still stands gripping the haft of his primitive weapon. As the beast turns the spear turns also, and Nu is whipped about as a leaf at the extremity of a gale-tossed branch.

Striking and cavorting futilely the colossal feline leaps hither and thither in prodigious bounds as he strives to reach the taunting figure that remains ever just beyond the zone of those destroying talons. But presently Oo goes more slowly, and now he stops and crouches flat upon his belly. Slowly and cautiously he reaches outward and backward with one huge paw until the torturing spear is within his grasp.

Meanwhile the man screams taunts and insults into the face of his enemy, at the same time forcing the spear further and further into the vitals of the tiger, for he knows that once that paw encircles the spear's haft his chances for survival will be of the slenderest. He has seen that Oo is weakening from loss of blood, but there are many fighting minutes left in the big carcass unless a happy twist of the spear sends its point through the wall of the great heart.

But at length the beast succeeds. The paw closes upon the spear. The tough wood bends beneath the weight of those steel thews, then snaps short a foot from the tiger's body, and at the same instant Oo rears and throws himself upon the youth, who has snatched his stone hunting knife from between his teeth and crouches, ready for the impact.

Down they go, the man entirely buried beneath the great body of his antagonist. Again and again the crude knife is buried in the snowy breast of the tiger even while Nu is falling beneath the screaming, tearing incarnation of bestial rage.

At the instant it strikes the man as strange that not once have the snapping jaws or frightful talons touched him, and then he is crushed to earth beneath the dead weight of Oo. The beast gives one last, Titanic struggle, and is still.

With difficulty Nu wriggles from beneath the carcass of his kill. At the last moment the tiger itself had forced the spear's point into its own heart as it bent and broke the haft. The man leaps to his feet and cuts the great throat. Then, as the blood flows, he dances about the dead body of his vanquished foe, brandishing his knife and recovered hatchet, and emitting now shrill shrieks in mimicry of Oo, and now deep toned roars – the call of the victorious cave man.

From the surrounding cliffs and jungle came answering

challenges from a hundred savage throats – the rumbling thunder of the cave bear's growl; the roar of Zor, the lion; the wail of the hyena; the trumpeting of the mammoth; the deep toned bellowing of the bull bos, and from distant swamp and sea came the hissing and whistling of saurians and amphibians.

His victory dance completed, Nu busied himself in the removal of the broken spear from the carcass of his kill. At the same time he removed several strong tendons from Oo's fore arm, with which he roughly spliced the broken haft, for there was never an instant in the danger fraught existence of his kind when it was well to be without the service of a stone-tipped spear.

This precaution taken, the man busied himself with the task of cutting off Oo's head, that he might bear it in triumph to the cave of his love. With stone hatchet and knife he hacked and hewed for the better part of a half hour, until at last he raised the dripping trophy above his head, as, leaping high in air, he screamed once more the gloating challenge of the victor, that all the world might know that there was no greater hunter than Nu, the son of Nu.

Even as the last note of his fierce cry rolled through the heavy, humid, super-heated air of the Niocene there came a sudden hush upon the face of the world. A strange darkness obscured the swollen sun. The ground trembled and shook. Deep rumblings muttered upward from the bowels of the young earth, and answering grumblings thundered down from the firmament above.

The startled troglodyte looked quickly in every direction, searching for the great beast who could thus cause the whole land to tremble and cry out in fear, and the heavens above to moan, and the sun to hide itself in terror.

In every direction he saw frightened beasts and birds and flying reptiles scurrying in panic stricken terror in search of hiding places, and moved by the same primitive instinct the young giant grabbed up his weapons and his trophy, and ran like an antelope for the sheltering darkness of the cave of Oo.

Scarcely had he reached the fancied safety of the interior

when the earth's crust crumpled and rocked – there was a sickening sensation of sudden sinking, and amidst the awful roar and thunder of rending rock, the cave mouth closed, and in the impenetrable darkness of his living tomb Nu, the son of Nu, Nu of the Niocene, lost consciousness.

That was a hundred thousand years ago.

CHAPTER TWO

THE EARTHQUAKE

To have looked at her, merely, you would never have thought Victoria Custer, of Beatrice, Nebraska, at all the sort of girl she really was. Her large dreamy eyes, and the graceful lines of her slender figure gave one an impression of that physical cowardice which we have grown to take for granted as an inherent characteristic of the truly womanly woman. And yet I dare say there were only two things on God's green earth that Victoria Custer feared, or beneath it or above it, for that matter – mice and earthquakes.

She readily admitted the deadly terror which the former aroused within her; but of earthquakes she seldom if ever would speak. To her brother Barney, her chum and confidant, she had on one or two occasions unburdened her soul.

The two were guests now of Lord and Lady Greystoke upon the Englishman's vast estate in equatorial Africa, in the country of the Waziri, to which Barney Custer had come to hunt big game – and forget. But all that has nothing to do with this story; nor has John Clayton, Lord Greystoke, who was, once upon a time, Tarzan of the Apes, except that my having chanced to be a guest of his at the same time as the Custers makes it possible for me to give you a story that otherwise might never have been told.

South of Uziri, the country of the Waziri, lies a chain of rugged mountains at the foot of which stretches a broad plain where antelope, zebra, giraffe, rhino and elephant abound, and here are lion and leopard and hyena preying, each after his own fashion, upon the sleek, fat herds of antelope, zebra and giraffe. Here, too, are buffalo – irritable, savage beasts, more formidable than the lion himself Clayton says.

It is indeed a hunter's paradise, and scarce a day passed that did not find a party absent from the low, rambling bungalow of the Greystokes in search of game and adventure, nor seldom was it that Victoria Custer failed to be of the party.

Already she had bagged two leopards, in addition to numerous antelope and zebra, and on foot had faced a bull buffalo's charge, bringing him down with a perfect shot within ten paces of where she stood.

At first she had kept her brother in a state bordering on nervous collapse, for the risks she took were such as few men would care to undertake; but after he had discovered that she possessed perfect coolness in the face of danger, and that the accuracy of her aim was so almost uncanny as to wring unstinted praise from the oldest hunters among them he commenced to lean a trifle too far in the other direction, so that Victoria was often in positions where she found herself entirely separated from the other members of the party – a compliment to her prowess which she greatly prized, since women and beginners were usually surrounded by precautions and guards through which it was difficult to get within firing distance of any sort of game.

As they were riding homeward one evening after a hunt in the foothills Barney noticed that his sister was unusually quiet, and apparently depressed.

'What's the matter, Vic?' he asked. 'Dead tired, eh?'

The girl looked up with a bright smile, which was immediately followed by an expression of puzzled bewilderment.

'Barney,' she said, after a moment of silence, 'there is something about those hills back there that fills me with the strangest sensation of terror imaginable. Today I passed an outcropping of volcanic rock that gave evidence of a frightful convulsion of nature in some bygone age. At sight of it I commenced to tremble from head to foot, a cold perspiration breaking out all over me. But that part is not so strange – you know I have always been subject to these same silly attacks of unreasoning terror at sight of any evidence of the mighty forces that have wrought changes in the earth's crust, or of the slightest tremor of an earthquake; but today the feeling of unutterable personal loss which overwhelmed me was almost unbearable – it was as though one whom I loved above all others had been taken from me.

'And yet,' she continued, 'through all my inexplicable sorrow there shone a ray of brilliant hope as remarkable and unfathomable as the deeper and depressing emotion which still stirred me.'

For some time neither spoke, but rode silently stirrup to stirrup as their ponies picked their ways daintily through the knee high grass. The girl was thinking – trying to puzzle out an explanation of the rather weird sensations which had so recently claimed her. Barney Custer was one of those unusual and delightful people who do not scoff at whatever they cannot understand; the reason, doubtless, that his sister as well as others chose him as the recipient of their confidences. Not understanding her emotion he had nothing to offer, and so remained silent. He was, however, not a little puzzled, as he had always been at each new manifestation of Victoria's uncanny reaction to every indication of the great upheavals which marked the physical changes in the conformation of the earth's crust.

He recalled former occasions upon which his sister had confided in him something of similar terrors. Once in The Garden of the Gods, and again during a trip through The Grand Canyon in Arizona, and very vivid indeed was the recollection of Victoria's nervous collapse following the reading of the press despatches describing the San Francisco earthquake. In all other respects his sister was an exceptionally normal well-balanced young American woman – which fact, doubtless, rendered her one weakness the more apparent.

But Victoria Custer's terror of earthquakes was not her

only peculiarity. The other was her strange contempt for the men who had sued for her hand – and these had been many. Her brother had thought several of them the salt of the earth, and Victoria had liked them, too, but as for loving them? Perish the thought!

Oddly enough recollection of this other phase of her character obtruded itself upon Barney's memory as the two rode on toward the Clayton bungalow, and with it he recalled a persistent dream which Victoria had said recurred after each reminder of a great convulsion of nature. At the thought he broke the silence.

'Has your – ah – avatar made his customary appearance?' he asked, smiling.

The girl extended her hand toward her brother and laid it on his where it rested upon his thigh as he rode, looking up at him with half frightened, half longing eyes.

'Oh, Barney,' she cried, 'you are such a dear never to have laughed at my silly dreams. I'm sure I should go quite mad did I not have you in whom to confide; but lately I have hesitated to speak of it even to you – he has been coming so often! Every night since we first hunted in the vicinity of the hills I have walked hand in hand with him beneath a great equatorial moon beside a restless sea, and more clearly than ever in the past have I seen his form and features. He is very handsome, Barney, and very tall and strong, and clean limbed – I wish that I might meet such a man in real life. I know it is a ridiculous thing to say, but I can never love any of the pusillanimous weaklings who are forever falling in love with me – not after having walked hand in hand with such as he and read the love in his clear eyes. And yet, Barney, I am afraid of him. Is it not odd?'

At this juncture they were joined by other members of the party, so that no further reference to the subject was made by either. At the Claytons they found that an addition had been made to the number of guests by the unheralded advent of two khaki clad young men, one of whom rose and came forward to meet the returning hunters while they were yet a hundred yards away.

He was a tall, athletic appearing man. As Victoria Custer

recognized his features she did not know whether to be pleased or angry. Here was the one man she had ever met who came nearest to the realization of her dream-man, and this one of all the others had never spoken a word of love to her. His companion who had now risen from the cool shade of the low veranda was also coming forward, but more slowly, the set of his shoulders and the swing of his stride betokening his military vocation.

'Mr Curtiss!' exclaimed Victoria, and looking past him, 'and Lieutenant Butzow! Where in the world did you come from?'

'The world left us,' replied the officer, smiling, 'and we have followed her to the wilds of Equatorial Africa.'

'We found Nebraska a very tame place after you and Barney left,' explained Mr Curtiss, 'and when I discovered that Butzow would accompany me we lost no time in following you, and here we are throwing ourselves upon the mercy and hospitality of Lady Greystoke.'

'I have been trying to convince them,' said that lady, who had now joined the party at the foot of the veranda steps, 'that the obligation is all upon our side. It taxes our ingenuity and the generosity of our friends to keep the house even half full of congenial companions.'

It was not until after dinner that night that Mr William Curtiss had an opportunity to draw Miss Victoria Custer away from the others upon some more or less hazy pretext that he might explain for her ears alone just why he had suddenly found Beatrice, Nebraska, such a desolate place and had realized that it was imperative to the salvation of his life and happiness that he travel halfway around the world in search of a certain slender bit of femininity.

This usually self-possessed young man stammered and hesitated like a bashful school boy speaking his Friday afternoon piece; but finally he managed to expel from his system, more or less coherently, the fact that he was very much in love with Victoria Custer, and that he should never again eat or sleep until she had promised to be his wife.

There was a strong appeal to the girl in the masterful thing the man had done in searching her out in the wilds of

Africa to tell her of his love, for it seemed that he and Butzow had forced their way with but a handful of carriers through a very savage section of the savage jungle because it was the shortest route from the coast to the Greystoke ranch.

Then there was that about him which appealed to the same attribute of her nature to which the young giant of her dreams appealed – a primitive strength and masterfulness that left her both frightened and happily helpless in the presence of both these strong loves, for the love of her dream man was to Victoria Custer a real and living love.

Curtiss saw assent in the silence which followed his outbreak, and taking advantage of this tacit encouragement, he seized her hands in his and drew her toward him.

'Oh, Victoria,' he whispered, 'tell me that thing I wish to hear from your dear lips. Tell me that even a tenth part of my love is returned, and I shall be happy.'

She looked up into his eyes, shining down upon her in the moonlight, and on her lips trembled an avowal of the love she honestly believed she could at last bestow upon the man of her choice. In the past few moments she had thrashed out the question of that other, unreal and intangible love that had held her chained to a dream for years, and in the cold light of twentieth century American rationality she had found it possible to put her hallucinations from her and find happiness in the love of this very real and very earnest young man.

'Billy,' he said, 'I—' but she got no further. Even as the words that would have bound her to him were forming upon her tongue there came a low sullen rumbling from the bowels of the earth – the ground rose and fell beneath them as the swell of the sea rises and falls. Then there came a violent trembling and shaking and a final deafening crash in the distance that might have accompanied the birth of mountain ranges.

With a little moan of terror the girl drew away from Curtiss, and then, before he could restrain her, she had turned and fled toward the bungalow. At the veranda steps she was met by the other members of the house party, and by the Greystokes and numerous servants who had rushed out at the first premonition of the coming shock.

Barney Custer saw his sister running toward the house, and knowing her terror of such phenomena ran to meet her. Close behind her came Curtiss, just in time to see the girl swoon in her brother's arms. Barney carried her to her room, where Lady Greystoke, abandoning the youthful 'Jack' to his black mammy, Esmeralda, ministered to her.

CHAPTER THREE

NU THE SLEEPER AWAKES

The shock that had been felt so plainly in the valley had been much more severe in the mountains to the south. In one place an overhanging cliff had split and fallen away from the face of the mountain, bumbling with a mighty roar into the valley below. As it hurtled down the mountainside the moonlight shining upon the fresh scar that it had left behind it upon the hill's face revealed the mouth of a gloomy cave from which there tumbled the inert figure of an animal which rolled down the steep declivity in the wake of the mass of rock that had preceded it – the tearing away of which had opened up the cavern in which it had lain.

For a hundred feet perhaps the body rolled, coming to a stop upon a broad ledge. For some time it lay perfectly motionless, but at last a feeble movement of the limbs was discernible. Then for another long period it was quiet. Minutes dragged into hours and still the lonely thing lay upon the mountainside, while upon the plain below it hungry lions moaned and roared, and all the teeming life of the savage wilds took up their search for food, their sleeping and their love-making where they had dropped them in the fright of the earthquake.

At last the stars paled and the eastern horizon glowed to a new day, and then the thing upon the ledge sat up. It was a man. Still partially dazed he drew his hand across his eyes and looked about him in bewilderment. Then, staggering a little, he rose to his feet, and as he came erect, the new sun shining on his bronzed limbs and his shock of black hair, roughly cropped between sharpened stones, his youth and beauty became startlingly apparent.

He looked about him upon the ground, and not finding that which he sought turned his eyes upward toward the mountain until they fell upon the cave mouth he had just quitted so precipitately. Quickly he clambered back to the cavern, his stone hatchet and knife beating against his bare hips as he climbed. For a moment he was lost to view within the cave, but presently he emerged, in one hand a stone-tipped spear, which seemed recently to have been broken and roughly spliced with raw tendons, and in the other the severed head of an enormous beast, which more nearly resembled the royal tiger of Asia than it did any other beast, though that resemblance was little closer than is the resemblance of the Royal Bengal to a house kitten.

The young man was Nu, the son of Nu. For a hundred thousand years he had lain hermetically sealed in his rocky tomb, as toads remain in suspended animation for similar periods of time. The earthquake had unsealed his sepulcher, and the rough tumble down the mountainside had induced respiration. His heart had responded to the pumping of his lungs, and simultaneously the other organs of his body had taken up their various functions as though they had never ceased functioning.

As he stood upon the threshold of the cave of Oo, the man hunter, the look of bewilderment grew upon his features as his eyes roved over the panorama of the unfamiliar world which lay spread below him. There was scarce an object to remind him of the world that had been but a brief instant before, for Nu could not know that ages had rolled by since he took hasty refuge in the lair of the great beast he had slain.

He thought that he might be dreaming, and so he rubbed his eyes and looked again; but still he saw the unfamiliar trees and bushes about him and further down in the valley the odd appearing vegetation of the jungle. Nu could not fathom the mystery of it. Slowly he stepped from the cave and began the descent toward the valley, for he was very thirsty and very hungry. Below him he saw animals grazing upon the broad plain, but even at that distance he realized that they were such as no mortal eye had ever before rested upon.

Warily he advanced, every sense alert against whatever new form of danger might lurk in this strange, new world. Had he had any conception of a life after death he would doubtless have felt assured that the earthquake had killed him and that he was now wandering through the heavenly vale; but the men of Nu's age had not yet conceived any sort of religion, other than a vague fear of certain natural phenomena such as storms and earthquakes, the movements of the sun and moon, and those familiar happenings which first awake the questionings of the primitive.

He saw the sun; but to him it was a different sun from the great, swollen orb that had shone through the thick, humid atmosphere of the Niocene. From Oo's lair only the day before he had been able to see in the distance the shimmering surface of the restless sea; but now as far as eye could reach there stretched an interminable jungle of gently waving tree tops, except for the rolling plain at his feet where yesterday the black jungle of the ape-people had reared its lofty fronds.

Nu shook his head. It was all quite beyond him; but there were certain things which he could comprehend, and so, after the manner of the self-reliant, he set about to wrest his livelihood from nature under the new conditions which had been imposed upon him while he slept.

First of all his spear must be attended to. It would never do to trust to that crude patch longer than it would take him to find and fit a new haft. His meat must wait until that thing was accomplished. In the meantime he might pick up what fruit was available in the forest toward which he was bending his steps in search of a long, straight shoot of the hard wood which alone would meet his requirements. In the days that had been Nu's there had grown in isolated patches a few lone clumps of very straight, hard-wood trees. The smaller of these the men of the tribe would cut down and split lengthways with stone wedges until from a single tree they might have produced material for a score or more spear shafts; but now Nu must see the very smallest of saplings, for he had no time to waste in splitting a larger tree, even had he had the necessary wedges and hammers.

Into the forest the youth crept, for though a hundred thousand years had elapsed since his birth he was still to all intent and purpose a youth. Upon all sides he saw strange and wonderful trees, the likes of which had never been in the forests of yesterday. The growths were not so luxuriant or prodigious, but for the most part the trees offered suggestions of alluring possibilities to the semiarboreal Nu, for the branches were much heavier and more solid than those of the great tree-ferns of his own epoch, and commenced much nearer the ground. Cat-like he leaped into the lower branches of them, revelling in the ease with which he could travel from tree to tree.

Gay colored birds of strange appearance screamed and scolded at him. Little monkeys hurried, chattering, from his path. Nu laughed. What a quaint, diminutive world it was indeed! Nowhere had he yet seen a tree or creature that might compare in size to the monsters among which he had traveled the preceding day.

The fruits, too, were small and strange. He scarcely dared venture to eat of them lest they be poisonous. If the lesser ape folk would only let him come close enough to speak with them he might ascertain from them which were safe, but for some unaccountable reason they seemed to fear and mistrust him. This above all other considerations argued to Nu that he had come in some mysterious way into another world.

Presently the troglodyte discovered a slender, straight young sapling. He came to the ground and tested its strength by bending it back and forth. Apparently it met the requirements of a new shaft. With his stone hatchet he hewed it off close to the ground, stripped it of branches, and climbing to the safety of the trees again, where he need fear no interruption from the huge monsters of the world he knew, set to work with his stone knife to remove the bark and shape the end to receive his spear head. First he split it down the center for four or five inches, and then he cut notches in the surface upon either side of the split portion. Now he carefully unwraps the rawhide that binds the spear head into his old shaft, and for want of water to moisten it crams the whole unfragrant mass into his mouth that it may be softened by warmth and saliva. For several minutes he busies himself in shaping the point of the new shaft that it may exactly fit the inequalities in the shank of the spear head. By the time this is done the rawhide had been sufficiently moistened to permit him to wind it tightly about the new haft into which he has set the spear head.

As he works he hears the noises of the jungle about him. There are many familiar voices, but more strange ones. Not once has the cave bear spoken; nor Zor, the mighty lion of the Niocene; nor Oo, the saber-toothed tiger. He misses the bellowing of the bull bos, and the hissing and whistling of monster saurian and amphibian. To Nu it seems a silent world. Propped against the bole of the tree before him grins the hideous head of the man hunter, the only familiar object in all this strange, curiously changed world about him.

Presently he becomes aware that the lesser apes are creeping warily closer to have a better look at him. He waits silently until from the tail of his eye he glimpses one quite near, and then in a low voice he speaks in the language that his allies of yesterday understood, and though ages had elapsed since that long gone day the little monkey above him understood, for the language of the apes can never change.

'Why do you fear Nu, the son of Nu?' asked the man. 'When has he ever harmed the ape-people?'

'The hairless ones kill us with sharp sticks that fly through the air,' replied the monkey; 'or with sticks that make a great noise and kill us from afar; but you seem not to be of these. We have never seen one like you until now. Do you not wish to kill us?'

'Why should I?' replied Nu. 'It is better that we be friends. All that I wish of you is that you tell me which of the fruits that grow here be safe for me to eat, and then direct me to the sea beside which dwell the tribe of Nu, my father.'

The monkeys had gathered in force by this time, seeing that the strange white ape offered no harm to their fellows and when they learned his wants they scampered about in all directions to gather nuts and fruits and berries for him. It is true that some of them forgot what they had intended doing before the task was half completed, and ended by pulling one another's tails and frolicking among the higher branches, or else ate the fruit they had gone to gather for their new friend; but a few there were with greater powers of concentration than their fellows who returned with fruit and berries and caterpillars, all of which Nu devoured with the avidity of the half-famished.

Of the whereabouts of the tribe of his father they could tell him nothing, for they had never heard of such a people, or of the great sea beside which he told them that his people dwelt.

His breakfast finished, and his spear repaired Nu set out toward the plain to bring down one of the beasts he had seen grazing there, for his stomach called aloud for flesh. Fruit and bugs might be all right for children and ape-people; but a full grown man must have meat, warm and red and dripping.

Closest to him as he emerged from the jungle browsed a small herd of zebra. They were directly up wind, and between him and them were patches of tall grass and clumps of trees scattered about the surface of the plain. Nu wondered at the strange beasts, admiring their gaudy markings as he came closer to them. Upon the edge of the herd nearest him a plump stallion stood switching his tail against the annoying flies, occasionally raising his head from his feeding to search the horizon for signs of danger, sniffing the air for the tell-tale scent of an enemy. It was he that Nu selected for his prey.

Stealthily the cave man crept through the tall grass, scarce a blade moving to the sinuous advance of his sleek body. Within fifty feet of the zebra Nu stopped, for the stallion was giving evidence of restlessness, as though sensing intuitively the near approach of a foe he could neither see, nor hear, nor smell.

The man, still prone upon his belly, drew his spear into the throwing grasp. With utmost caution he wormed his legs beneath him, and then, like lightning and all with a single movement, he leaped to his feet and cast the stone-tipped weapon at his quarry.

With a snort of terror the stallion reared to plunge away, but the spear had found the point behind his shoulder even as he saw the figure of the man arise from the tall grasses, and as the balance of the herd galloped madly off, their leader pitched headlong to the earth.

Nu ran forward with ready knife, but the animal was dead before he reached its side – the great spear had passed through its heart and was protruding upon the opposite side of the body. The man removed the weapon, and with his knife cut several long strips of meat from the plump haunches.

Ever and anon he raised his head to scan the plain and jungle for evidences of danger, sniffing the breeze just as had the stallion he had killed. His work was but partially completed when he caught the scent of man yet a long way off. He knew that he could not be mistaken, yet never had he sensed so strange an odor. There were men coming, he knew, but of the other odors that accompanied them he could make nothing, for khaki and guns and sweaty saddle blankets and the stench of tanned leather were to Nu's nostrils as Greek would have been to his ears.

It would be best thought Nu to retreat to the safety of the forest until he could ascertain the number and kind of beings that were approaching, and so, taking but careless advantage of the handier shelter, the cave man sauntered toward the forest, for now he was not stalking game, and never yet had he shown fear in the presence of an enemy. If their numbers were too great for him to cope with single handed he would not show himself; but none might ever say that he had seen Nu, the son of Nu, run away from danger.

In his hand still swung the head of Oo, and as the man leaped to the low branches of a tree at the jungle's edge to spy upon the men he knew to be advancing from the far side of the plain, he fell to wondering how he was to find his way back to Nat-ul that he might place the trophy at her feet and claim her as his mate.

Only the previous evening they had walked together hand in hand along the beach, and now he had not the remotest conception of where that beach lay. Straight across the plain should be the direction of it, for from that direction had he come to find the lair of Oo! But now all was changed. There was no single familiar landmark to guide him, not even the ape-people knew of any sea nearby, and he himself had no conception as to whether he was in the same world that he had traversed when last the sun shone upon him.

CHAPTER FOUR

THE MYSTERIOUS HUNTER

The morning following the earthquake found Victoria Custer still confined to her bed. She told Lady Greystoke that she felt weak from the effects of the nervous shock; but the truth of the matter was that she dreaded to meet Curtiss and undergo the ordeal which she knew confronted her.

How was she to explain to him the effect that the subterranean rumblings and the shaking of the outer crust had had upon her and her sentiments toward him? When her brother came in to see her she drew his head down upon the pillow beside hers and whispered something of the terrible hallucinations that had haunted her since the previous evening.

'Oh, Barney,' she cried, 'what can it be? What can it be? The first deep grumblings that preceded the shock seemed to awake me as from a lethargy, and as plainly as I see you beside me now, I saw the half naked creature of my dreams, and when I saw him I knew that I could never wed Mr Curtiss or any other – it is awful to have to admit it even to you, Barney, but I – I knew when I saw him that I loved him – that I was his. Not his wife, Barney, but his woman – his mate, and I had to fight with myself to keep from rushing out into the terrible blackness of the night to throw myself into his arms. It was then that I managed to control myself long enough to run to you, where I fainted. And last night, in my dreams, I saw him again, – alone and lonely, searching through a strange and hostile world to find and claim me.

'You cannot know, Barney, how real he is to me. It is not as other dreams, but instead I really see him – the satin texture of his smooth, bronzed skin; the lordly poise of his perfect head; the tousled shock of coal black hair that I have learned to love and through which I know I have run my fingers as he stooped to kiss me.

'He carries a great spear, stone-tipped – I should know it the moment that I saw it – and a knife and hatchet of the same flinty material, and in his left hand he bears the severed head of a mighty beast.

'He is a noble figure, but of another world or of another age; and somewhere he wanders so lonely and alone that my heart weeps at the thought of him. Oh, Barney, either he is true and I shall find him, or I am gone mad. Tell me Barney, for the love of heaven! you believe that I am sane.'

Barney Custer drew his sister's face close to his and kissed her tenderly.

'Of course you're sane, Vic,' he reassured her. 'You've just allowed that old dream of yours to become a sort of obsession with you, and now it's gotten on your nerves until you are commencing to believe it even against your better judgment. Take a good grip on yourself, get up and join Curtiss in a long ride. Have it out with him. Tell him just what you have told me, and then tell him you'll marry him, and I'll warrant that you'll be dreaming about him instead of that young giant that you have stolen out of some fairy tale.'

'I'll get up and take a ride, Barney,' replied the girl; 'but as for marrying Mr Curtiss – well, I'll have to think it over.'

But after all she did not join the party that was riding toward the hills that morning, for the thought of seeing the torn and twisted strata of a bygone age that lifted its scarred head above the surface of the plain at the base of the mountains was more than she felt equal to. They did not urge her, and as she insisted that Mr Curtiss accompany the other men she was left alone at the bungalow with Lady Greystoke, the baby and the servants.

As the party trotted across the rolling land that stretched before them to the foothills they sighted a herd of zebras coming toward them in mad stampede.

'Something is hunting ahead of us,' remarked one of the men.

'We may get a shot at a lion from the looks of it,' replied another.

A short distance further on they came upon the carcass of a zebra stallion. Barney and Butzow dismounted to examine it in an effort to determine the nature of the enemy that had despatched it. At the first glance Barney called to one of the other members of the party, an experienced big game hunter.

'What do you make of this, Brown?' he asked, pointing to the exposed haunch.

'It is a man's kill,' replied the other. 'Look at that gaping hole over the heart, that would tell the story were it not for the evidence of the knife that cut away these strips from the rump. The carcass is still warm – the kill must have been made within the past few minutes.'

'Then it wouldn't have been a man,' spoke up another, 'or we should have heard the shot. Wait, here's Greystoke, let's see what he thinks of it.'

The ape man, who had been riding a couple of hundred yards in rear of the others with one of the older men, now reined in close to the dead zebra.

'What have we here?' he asked, swinging from his saddle.

'Brown says this looks the kill of a man,' said Barney; 'but none of us heard any shot.'

Tarzan grasped the zebra by a front and hind pastern and rolled him over upon his other side.

'It went way through, whatever it was,' said Butzow, as the hole behind this shoulder was exposed to view. 'Must have been a bullet even if we didn't hear the report of the gun.'

'I'm not so sure of that,' said Tarzan, and then he glanced casually at the ground about the carcass, and bending lower brought his sensitive nostrils close to the mutilated haunch and then to the tramped grasses at the zebra's side. When he straightened up the others looked at him questioningly.

'A man,' he said – 'a white man, has been here since the zebra died. He cut these steaks from the haunches. There is not the slightest odor of gun powder about the wound – it was not made by a powder-sped projectile. It is too large and too deep for an arrow wound. The only other weapon that could have inflicted it is a spear; but to cast a spear entirely through the carcass of a zebra at the distance to which a man could approach one in the open presupposes a mightiness of muscle and an accuracy of aim little short of super-human.'

'And you think—?' commenced Brown.

'I think nothing,' interrupted Tarzan, 'except that my judgment tells me that my senses are in error – there is no naked, white giant hunting through the country of the Waziri. Come, let's ride on to the hills and see if we can't locate the old villain who has been stealing my sheep. From his spoor I'll venture to say that when we bring him down we shall see the largest lion that any of us has ever seen.'

CHAPTER FIVE

THE WATCHER

As the party remounted and rode away toward the foothills two wondering black eyes watched them from the safety of the jungle. Nu was utterly non-plussed. What sort of men were these who rode upon beasts the like of which Nu had never dreamed? At first he thought their pith helmets and khaki clothing a part of them; but when one of them removed his helmet and another unbuttoned his jacket Nu saw that they were merely coverings for the head and body, though why men should wish to hamper themselves with such foolish and cumbersome contraptions the troglodyte could not imagine.

As the party rode toward the foothills Nu paralleled them, keeping always down wind from them. He followed them all day during their fruitless search for the lion that had been entering Greystoke's compound and stealing his sheep, and as they retraced their way toward the bungalow late in the afternoon Nu followed after them.

Never in his life had he been so deeply interested in anything as he was in these strange creatures, and when, half-way across the plain, the party came unexpectedly upon a band of antelope grazing in a little hollow and Nu heard the voice of one of the little black sticks the men carried and saw a buck leap into the air and then come heavily to the ground quite dead, deep respect was added to his interest, and possibly a trace of awe as well – fear he knew not.

In a clump of bushes a quarter of a mile from the bungalow Nu came to a halt. The strange odors that assailed his nostrils as he approached the ranch warned him to caution. The black servants and the Waziri warriors, some of whom were always visiting their former chief, presented to Nu's nostrils an unfamiliar scent – one which made the black shock upon his head stiffen as you have seen the hair upon the neck of a white man's hound stiffen when for the first time his nose detects the odor of an Indian. And, half smothered in the riot of more powerful odors, there came to Nu's nostrils now and then a tantalizing suggestion of a faint aroma that set his heart to pounding and the red blood coursing through his veins.

Never did it abide for a sufficient time to make Nu quite sure that it was more than a wanton trick of his senses – the result of the great longing that was in his lonely heart for her whom this ephemeral and elusive effluvium proclaimed. As darkness came he approached closer to the bungalow, always careful, however, to keep down wind from it.

Through the windows he could see people moving about within the lighted interior, but he was not close enough to distinguish features. He saw men and women sitting about a long table, eating with strange weapons upon which they impaled tiny morsels of food which lay upon round, flat stones before them.

There was much laughter and talking, which floated through the open windows to the cave man's eager ears; but throughout it all there came to him no single word which he could interpret. After these men and women had eaten they came out and sat in the shadows before the entrance to their strange cave, and here again they laughed and chattered, for all the world, thought Nu, like the ape-people; and yet, though it was different from the ways of his own people the troglodyte could not help but note within his own breast a strange yearning to take part in it – a longing for the company of these strange, new people.

He had crept quite close to the veranda now, and presently there floated down to him upon the almost stagnant air a subtle exhalation that is not precisely scent, and for which the languages of modern men have no expression since men themselves have no powers of perception which may grasp it; but to Nu of the Niocene it carried as clear and unmistakable a message as could word of mouth, and it told him that Nat-ul, the daughter of Tha, sat among these strange people before the entrance to their wonderful cave.

And yet Nu could not believe the evidence of his own senses. What could Nat-ul be doing among such as these? How, between two suns, could she have learned the language and the ways of these strangers? It was impossible; and then a man upon the veranda, who sat close beside Victoria Custer, struck a match to light a cigarette, and the flare of the blaze lit up the girl's features. At the sight of them the cave man involuntarily sprang to his feet. A half smothered exclamation broke from his lips: 'Nat-ul!'

'What was that?' exclaimed Barney Custer. 'I thought I heard some one speak out there near the rose bushes.'

He rose as though to investigate, but his sister laid her hand upon his arm.

'Don't go, Barney,' she whispered.

He turned toward her with a questioning look.

'Why?' he asked. 'There is no danger. Did you not hear it, too?'

'Yes,' she answered in a low voice, 'I heard it, Barney – please don't leave me.'

He felt the trembling of her hand where it rested upon his sleeve. One of the other men heard the conversation, but of course he could not guess that it carried any peculiar significance – it was merely an expression of the natural timidity of the civilized white woman in the midst of the savage African night.

'It's nothing, Miss Custer,' he said. 'I'll just walk down there to reassure you – a prowling hyena, perhaps, but nothing more.'

The girl would have been glad to deter him, but she felt that she had already evinced more perturbation than the occasion warranted, and so she but forced a laugh, remarking that it was not at all worth while, yet in her ears rang the familiar name that had so often fallen from the lips of her dream man.

When one of the others suggested that the investigator had better take an express rifle with him on the chance that the intruder might be 'old Raffles', the sheep thief, the girl started up as though to object but realizing how ridiculous such an attitude would be, and how impossible to explain, she turned instead and entered the house.

Several of the men walked down into the garden, but though they searched for the better part of half an hour they came upon no indication that any savage beast was nearby. Always in front of them a silent figure moved just outside the range of their vision, and when they returned again to the veranda it took up its position once more behind the rose bushes, nor until all had entered the bungalow and sought their beds did the figure stir.

Nu was hungry again, and knowing no law of property rights he found the odor of the Greystoke sheep as appetizing as that of any other of the numerous creatures that were penned within their compounds for the night. Like a supple panther the man scaled the high fence that guarded the imported, pedigreed stock in which Lord Greystoke took such just pride. A moment later there was the frightened rush of animals to the far side of the enclosure, where they halted to turn fear filled eyes back toward the silent beast of prey that crouched over the carcass of a plump ewe. Within the pen Nu ate his fill, and then, cat-like as he had come, he glided back stealthily toward the garden before the darkened bungalow.

Out across the plain, down wind from Nu, another silent figure moved stealthily toward the ranch. It was a huge, maned lion. Every now and then he would halt and lift his sniffing nose to the gentle breeze, and his lips would lift baring the mighty fangs beneath, but no sound came from his deep throat, for he was old, and his wisdom was as the wisdom of the fox.

Once upon a time he would have coughed and moaned and roared after the manner of his hungry brethren, but much experience with men-people and their deafening thunder sticks had taught him that he hunted longest who hunted in silence.

CHAPTER SIX

NU AND THE LION

Victoria Custer had gone to her room much earlier in the evening than was her custom, but not to sleep. She did not even disrobe, but sat instead in the darkness beside her window looking out toward the black and mysterious jungle in the distance, and the shadowy outlines of the southern hills.

She was trying to fight down forever the foolish obsession that had been growing upon her slowly and insidiously for years. Since the first awakening of developing womanhood within her she had been subject to the strange dream that was now becoming an almost nightly occurrence. At first she had thought nothing of it, other than it was odd that she should continue to dream the same thing so many times; but of late these nightly visions had seemed to hold more of reality than formerly, and to presage some eventful happening in her career – some crisis that was to alter the course of her life. Even by day she could not rid herself of the vision of the black haired young giant, and tonight the culmination had come when she had heard his voice calling her from the rose thicket. She knew that he was but a creature of her dreams, and it was this knowledge which frightened her so – for it meant but one thing; her mind was tottering beneath the burden of the nervous strain these hallucinations had imposed upon it.

She must gather all the resources of her nervous energy and throw off this terrible obsession forever. She must! She *must*! Rising, the girl paced back and forth the length of her room. She felt stifled and confined within its narrow limits. Outside, beneath the open sky, with no boundaries save the distant horizon was the place best fitted for such a battle as was raging within her. Snatching up a silken scarf she threw it about her shoulders – a concession to habit, for the night was hot – and stepping through her window to the porch that encircled the bungalow she passed on into the garden.

Just around the nearest angle of the house her brother and Billy Curtiss sat smoking before the window of their bed room, clad in pajamas and slippers. Curtiss was cleaning the rifle he had used that day – the same that he had carried into the rose garden earlier in the evening. Neither heard the girl's light footsteps upon the sward, and the corner of the building hid her from their view.

In the open moonlight beside the rose thicket Victoria Custer paced back and forth. A dozen times she reached a determination to seek the first opportunity upon the morrow to give Billy Curtiss an affirmative answer to the question he had asked her the night before – the night of the earthquake; but each time that she thought she had disposed of the matter definitely she found herself involuntarily comparing him with the heroic figure of her dream-man, and again she must need rewage her battle.

As she walked in the moonlight two pairs of eyes watched her every movement – one pair, clear, black eyes, from the rose thicket – the other flaming yellow-green orbs hidden in a little clump of bushes at the point where she turned in her passing to retrace her steps – at the point farthest from the watcher among the roses.

Twenty times Nu was on the point of leaping from his concealment and taking the girl in his arms, for to him she was Nat-ul, daughter of Tha, and it had not been a hundred thousand years, but only since the day before yesterday that he had last seen her. Yet each time something deterred him – a strange, vague, indefinable fear of this wondrous creature who was Nat-ul, and yet who was not Nat-ul, but another made in Nat-ul's image.

The strange things that covered her fair form seemed to have raised a barrier between them – the last time that he had walked hand in hand with her upon the beach naught but a soft strip of the skin of a red doe's calf had circled her gracefully undulating hips. Her familiar association, too, with these strange people, coupled with the fact that she spoke and understood their language only tended to remove her further from him. Nu was very sad, and very lonely; and the sight of Nat-ul seemed to accentuate rather than relieve his depression. Slowly there was born within him the conviction that Nat-ul was no longer for Nu, the son of Nu. Why, he could not guess; but the bitter fact seemed irrevocable.

The girl had turned quite close to him now, and was retracing her steps toward the bushes twenty yards away. Behind their screening verdure 'old Raffles' twitched his tufted tail and drew his steel thewed legs beneath him for the spring, and as he waited just the faintest of purrs escaped his slavering jowls. Too faint the sound to pierce the dulled senses of the twentieth century maiden; but to the man hiding in the rose thicket twenty paces further from the lion than she it fell deep and sinister upon his unspoiled ear.

Like a bolt of lightning – so quickly his muscles responded to his will – the cave man hurtled the intervening rose bushes with a single bound, and, raised spear in hand, bounded after the unconscious girl. The great lion saw him coming, and lest he be cheated of his prey leaped into the moonlight before his intended victim was quite within the radius of his spring.

The beast emitted a horrid roar that froze the girl with terror, and then in the face of his terrific charge the figure of a naked giant leaped past her. She saw a great arm, wielding a mighty spear, hurl the weapon at the infuriated beast – and then she swooned.

As the savage note of the lion's roar broke the stillness of the quiet night Curtiss and Barney Custer sprang to their feet, running toward the side of the bungalow from which the sound had come. Curtiss grasped the rifle he had but just reloaded, and as he turned the corner of the building he caught one fleeting glimpse of something moving near the bushes fifty yards away. Raising his weapon he fired.

The whole household had been aroused by the lion's deep voice and the answering boom of the big rifle, so that scarcely a minute after Barney and Curtiss reached the side of the prostrate girl a score of white men and black were gathered about them.

The dead body of a huge lion lay scarce twenty feet from Victoria Custer, but a hurried examination of the girl brought unutterable relief to them all, for she was uninjured. Barney lifted her in his arms and carried her to her room while the others examined the dead beast. From the center of the breast a wooden shaft protruded, and when they had drawn this out, and it required the united efforts of four strong men to do it, they found that a stone-tipped spear had passed straight through the savage heart almost the full length of the brute's body.

'The zebra killer,' said Brown to Greystoke. The latter nodded his head.

'We must find him,' he said. 'He has rendered us a great service. But for him Miss Custer would not be alive now;' but though twenty men scouted the grounds and the plain beyond for several hours no trace of the killer of 'old Raffles' could be found, and the reason that they did not find him abroad was because he lay directly beneath their noses in a little clump of low, flowering shrubs, with a bullet wound in his head.

CHAPTER SEVEN

VICTORIA OBEYS THE CALL

The next morning the men were examining the stone headed spear upon the veranda just outside the breakfast room.

'It's the oddest thing of its kind I ever saw,' said Greystoke. 'I can almost swear that it was never made by any of the tribesmen of present day Africa. I once saw several similar heads, though, in the British Museum. They had been taken from the debris of a prehistoric cave dwelling.'

From the window of the breakfast room just behind them a wide eyed girl was staring in breathless wonderment at the rude weapon, which to her presented concrete evidence of the reality of the thing she had thought but another hallucination – the leaping figure of the naked man that had sprung past her into the face of the charging lion an instant before she had swooned. One of the men turned and saw her standing there.

'Ah, Miss Custer,' he exclaimed; 'no worse off this morning I see for your little adventure of last night. Here's a memento that your rescuer left behind him in the heart of "old Raffles". Would you like it?'

The girl stepped forward hiding her true emotions behind the mask of a gay smile. She took the spear of Nu, the son of Nu, in her hands, and her heart leaped in half savage pride as she felt the weight of the great missile.

'What a man he must be who wields such a mighty weapon!' she exclaimed. Barney Custer was watching his sister closely, for with the discovery of the spear in the lion's body had come the sudden recollection of Victoria's description of her dream-man – 'He carried a great spear, stone-tipped – I should know it the moment that I saw it—'

The young man stepped to his sister's side, putting an arm about her shoulders. She looked up into his face, and then in a low voice that was not audible to the others she whispered: 'It is his, Barney. I knew that I should know it.'

For some time the young man had been harassed by fears as to his sister's sanity. Now he was forced to entertain fears of an even more sinister nature, or else admit that he too had gone mad. If he were sane, then it was God's truth that somewhere in this savage land a savage white man roamed in search of Victoria. Now that he had found her would he not claim her? He shuddered at the thought. He must do something to avert a tragedy, and he must act at once. He drew Lord Greystoke to one side.

'Victoria and I must leave at once,' he said. 'The nervous strain of the earthquake and this last adventure have told upon her to such an extent that I fear we may have a very sick girl upon our hands if I do not get her back to civilization and home as quickly as possible.'

Greystoke did not attempt to offer any remonstrances. He, too, felt that it would be best for Miss Custer to go home. He had noted her growing nervousness with increasing apprehension. It was decided that they should leave on the morrow. There were fifty black carriers anxious to return to the coast, and Butzow and Curtiss readily signified their willingness to accompany the Nebraskan and his sister.

As he was explaining his decision to Victoria a black servant came excitedly to Lord Greystoke. He told of the finding of a dead ewe in the compound. The animal's neck had been broken, the man said, and several strips of meat cut from its haunches with a knife. Beside it in the soft mud of the enclosure the prints of an unshod human foot were plainly in evidence.

Greystoke smiled. 'The zebra killer again,' he said. 'Well, he is welcome to all he can eat.'

Before he had finished speaking, Brown, who had been nosing around in the garden, called to him from a little clump of bushes beside the spot where the lion's body had lain.

'Look here, Clayton,' he called. 'Here's something we overlooked in the darkness last night.'

The men upon the veranda followed Greystoke to the

garden. Behind them came Victoria Custer, drawn as though by a magnet to the spot where they had gathered.

In the bushes was a little pool of dried blood, and where the earth near the roots was free from sod there were several impressions of a bare foot.

'He must have been wounded,' exclaimed Brown, 'by Curtiss's shot. I doubt if the lion touched him – the beast must have died instantly the spear entered its heart. But where can he have disappeared to?'

Victoria Custer was examining the grass a little distance beyond the bushes. She saw what the others failed to see – a drop of blood now and then leading away in the direction of the mountains to the south. At the sight of it a great compassion welled in her heart for the lonely, wounded man who had saved her life and then staggered, bleeding, toward the savage wilderness from which he had come. It seemed to her that somewhere out there he was calling to her now, and that she must go.

She did not call the attention of the others to her discovery, and presently they all returned to the veranda, where Barney again took up the discussion of their plans for tomorrow's departure. The girl interposed no objections. Barney was delighted to see that she was apparently as anxious to return home as he was to have her – he had feared a flat refusal.

Barney had wanted to get a buffalo bull before he left, and when one of the Waziri warriors brought word that morning that there was a splendid herd a few miles north of the ranch, Victoria urged him to accompany the other men upon the hunt.

'I'll attend to the balance of the packing,' she said. 'There's not the slightest reason in the world why you shouldn't go.'

And so he went, and Victoria busied herself in the gathering together of the odds and ends of their personal belongings. All morning the household was alive with its numerous duties, but after luncheon while the heat of the day was greatest the bungalow might have been entirely deserted for any sign of life that there was about it. Lady Greystoke was taking her siesta, as were practically all of the servants. Victoria Custer had paused in her work to gaze out of her window toward the distant hills far to the south. At her side, nosing his muzzle into her palm, stood one of Lord Greystoke's great wolfhounds, Terkoz. He had taken a great fancy to Victoria Custer from the first and whenever permitted to do so remained close beside her.

The girl's heart filled with a great longing as she looked wistfully out toward the hills that she had so feared before. She feared them still, yet something there called her. She tried to fight against the mad desire with every ounce of her reason, but she was fighting against an unreasoning instinct that was far stronger than any argument she could bring to bear against it.

Presently the hound's cold muzzle brought forth an idea in her mind, and with it she cast aside the last semblance of attempted restraint upon her mad desire. Seizing her rifle and ammunition belt she moved noiselessly into the veranda. There she found a number of leashes hanging from a peg. One of these she snapped to the hound's collar. Unseen, she crossed the garden to the little patch of bushes where the dried blood was. Here she gathered up some of the brown stained earth and held it close to Terkoz's nose. Then she put her finger to the ground where the trail of blood led away toward the south.

'Here, Terkoz!' she whispered.

The beast gave a low growl as the scent of the new blood filled his nostrils, and with nose close to ground started off, tugging upon the leash, in the direction of the mountains upon the opposite side of the plain.

Beside him walked the girl, across her shoulder was slung a modern big game rifle, and in her left hand swung the stone-tipped spear of the savage mate she sought.

What motive prompted her act she did not even pause to consider. The results she gave not the slightest thought. It seemed the most natural thing in the world that she should be seeking this lonely, wounded man. Her place was at his side. He needed her – that was enough for her to know. She was no longer the pampered, petted child of an effete civilization. That any metamorphosis had taken place within her she did not dream, nor is it certain that any change had occurred, for who may say that it is such a far step from one incarnation to another however many countless years of man-measured time may have intervened?

Darkness had fallen upon the plain and the jungle and the mountain, and still Terkoz forged ahead, nose to ground, and beside him moved the slender figure of the graceful girl. Now the roar of a distant lion came faintly to her ears, answered, quite close, by the moaning of another – a sound that is infinitely more weird and terrifying than the deeper throated challenge. The cough of the leopard and the uncanny 'laughter' of hyenas added their evidence that the night-prowling carnivora were abroad.

The hair along the wolfhound's spine stiffened in a little ridge of bristling rage. The girl unslung her rifle, shifting the leash to the hand that carried the heavy spear of the troglodyte; but she was unafraid. Suddenly, just before her, a little band of antelope sprang from the grass in startled terror – there was a hideous roar, and a great body hurtled through the air to alight upon the rump of the hindmost of the herd. A single scream of pain and terror from the stricken animal, a succession of low growls and the sound of huge jaws crunching through flesh and bone, and then silence.

The girl made a slight detour to avoid the beast and its kill, passing a hundred yards above them. In the moonlight the lion saw her and the hound. Standing across his fallen prey, his flaming eyes glaring at the intruders, he rumbled his deep warning to them; but Victoria, dragging the growling Terkoz after her, passed on and the king of beasts turned to his feast.

It was fifteen minutes before Terkoz could relocate the trail, and then the two took up their lonely way once more. Into the foothills past the tortured strata of an ancient age it wound. At sight of the naked rock the girl shuddered, yet on and up she went until Terkoz halted, bristling and growling, before the inky entrance to a gloomy cave.

Holding the beast back Victoria peered within. Her eyes could not penetrate the Stygian darkness. Here, evidently, the trail ended, but of a sudden it occurred to her that she had only surmised that the bloody spoor they had been following was that of the man she sought. It was almost equally as probable that Curtiss's shot had struck 'old Raffles' mate and that after all she had followed the blood of a wounded lioness to the creature's rocky lair.

Bending low she listened, and at last there came to her ears a sound as of a body moving, and then heavy breathing, and a sigh.

'Nu!' she whispered. 'Is it you? I have come,' nor did it seem strange to her that she spoke in a strange tongue, no word of which she had ever heard in all her life before. For a moment there was silence, and then, weakly, from the depths of the cave a voice replied.

'Nat-ul!' It was barely a whisper.

Quickly the girl groped her way into the cavern, feeling before her with her hands, until she came to the prostrate form of a man lying upon the cold, hard rock. With difficulty she kept the growling wolfhound from his throat. Terkoz had found the prey that he had tracked, and he could not understand why he should not now be allowed to make the kill; but he was a well-trained beast, and at last at the girl's command he took up a position at the cave's mouth on guard.

Victoria kneeled beside the prostrate form of Nu, the son of Nu; but she was no longer Victoria Custer. It was Nat-ul, the daughter of Tha, who kneeled there beside the man she loved. Gently she passed her slim fingers across his forehead – it was burning with a raging fever. She felt the wound along the side of his head and shuddered. Then she raised him in her arms so that his head was pillowed in her lap, and stooping kissed his cheek.

Halfway down the mountainside, she recalled, there was a little spring of fresh, cold water. Removing her hunting jacket she rolled it into a pillow for the unconscious man, and then with Terkoz at her side clambered down the rocky way. Filling her hat with water she returned to the cave. All night she bathed the fevered head, and washed the ugly wound, at times squeezing a few refreshing drops between the hot lips.

At last the restless tossing of the wounded man ceased, and the girl saw that he had fallen into a natural sleep, and that the fever had abated. When the first rays of the rising sun relieved the gloom within the cavern Terkoz, rising to stretch himself, looked backward into the interior. He saw a black-haired giant sleeping quietly, his head pillowed upon a khaki hunting coat, and beside him sat the girl, her loosened hair tumbled about her shoulders and over the breast of the sleeping man upon which her own tired head had dropped in the sleep of utter exhaustion. Terkoz yawned and lay down again.

CHAPTER EIGHT

CAPTURED BY ARABS

After a time the girl awoke. For a few minutes she could not assure herself of the reality of her surroundings. She thought that this was but another of her dreams. Gently she put out her hand and touched the face of the sleeper. It was very real. Also she noted that the fever had left. She sat in silence for a few minutes attempting to adjust herself to the new and strange conditions which surrounded her. She seemed to be two people – the American girl, Victoria Custer, and Nat-ul; but who or from where was Nat-ul she could not fathom, other than that she was beloved by Nu and that she returned his love.

She wondered that she did not regret the life of ease she had abandoned, and which she knew that she could never again return to. She was still sufficiently of the twentieth century to realize that the step she had taken must cut her off forever from her past life – yet she was very happy. Bending low over the man she kissed his lips, and then rising went outside, and calling Terkoz with her descended to the spring, for she was thirsty.

Neither the girl nor the hound saw the white robed figures

that withdrew suddenly behind a huge boulder as the two emerged from the cave's mouth. Nor did they see him signal to others behind him who had not yet rounded the shoulder of the cliff at the base of which they had been marching.

Victoria stooped to fill her hat at the spring. First she leaned far down to quench her own thirst. A sudden, warning growl from Terkoz brought her head up, and there, not ten paces from her, she saw a dozen white robed Arabs, and behind them half a hundred blacks. All were armed – evil looking fellows they were, and one of the Arabs had covered her with his long gun.

Now he spoke to her, but in a tongue she did not understand, though she knew that his message was unfriendly, and imagined that it warned her not to attempt to use her own rifle which lay beside her. Next he spoke to those behind him and two of them approached the girl, one from either side, while the leader continued to keep his piece leveled at her.

As the two came toward her she heard a menacing growl from the wolfhound, and then saw him leap for the nearest Arab. The fellow clubbed his gun and swung it full upon Terkoz's skull, so that the faithful hound collapsed in a silent heap at their feet. Then the two rushed in and seized Victoria's rifle, and a moment later she was roughly dragged toward the leader of the ill-favored gang.

Through one of the blacks, a West Coast negro who had picked up a smattering of pidgin English, the leader questioned the girl, and when he found that she was a guest of Lord Greystoke an ugly grin crossed his evil face, for the fellow recalled what had befallen another Arab slave and ivory caravan at the hands of the Englishman and his Waziri warriors. Here was an opportunity for partial revenge. He motioned for his followers to bring her along – there was no time to tarry in this country of their enemies into which they had accidentally stumbled after being lost in the jungle for the better part of a month.

Victoria asked what their intentions toward her were; but all that she could learn was that they would take her north with them. She offered to arrange the payment of a suitable ransom if they would return her to her friends unharmed, but the Arab only laughed at her.

'You will bring a good price,' he said, 'at the court of the sultan of Fulad, north of Tagwara, and for the rest I shall have partly settled the score which I have against the Englishman,' and so Victoria Custer disappeared from the sight of men at the border of the savage land of the Waziri nor was there any other than her captors to know the devious route that they followed to gain the country north of Uziri.

When at last Nu, the son of Nu, opened his eyes from the deep slumber that had refreshed and invigorated him, he looked up expectantly for the sweet face that had been hovering above his, and as he realized that the cave was tenantless except for himself a sigh that was half a sob broke from the depth of his lonely heart, for he knew that Nat-ul had been with him only in his dreams.

Yet it had been so real! Even now he could feel the touch of her cool hand upon his forehead, and her slim fingers running through his hair. His cheek glowed to her hot kisses, and in his nostrils was the sweet aroma of her dear presence. The disillusionment of his waking brought with it bitter disappointment, and a return of the fever. Again Nu lapsed into semi-consciousness and delirium, so that he was not aware of the figure of the khaki clad white man that crept warily into the half-darkness of his lair shortly after noon.

It was Barney Custer, and behind him came Curtiss, Butzow and a half dozen others of the searching party. They had stumbled up the half dead Terkoz beside the spring, and there also they had found Victoria Custer's hat, and plainly in the soft earth between the bowlders of the hillside they had seen the new made path to the cave higher up.

When Barney saw that the prostrate figure within the cavern did not stir at his entrance a stifling fear rose in his throat, for he was sure that he had found the dead body of his sister; but as his eyes became more accustomed to the dim light of the interior he realized his mistake – at first with a sense of infinite relief and later with misgivings that amounted almost to a wish that it had been Victoria, safe in death; for among the savage men of savage Africa there are fates worse than death for women.

The others had crowded in beside him, and one had lighted a torch of dry twigs which illuminated the interior of the cave brightly for a few seconds. In that time they saw that the man was the only occupant and that he was helpless from fever. Beside him lay the stone spear that had slain 'old Raffles' – each of them recognized it. How could it have been brought to him?

'The zebra killer,' said Brown. 'What's that beneath his head? Looks like a khaki coat.'

Barney drew it out and held it up.

'God!' muttered Curtiss. 'It's hers.'

'He must 'ave come down there after we left, an' got his spear an' stole your sister,' said Brown.

Curtiss drew his revolver and pushed closer toward the unconscious Nu.

'The beast,' he growled; 'shootin's too damned good for him. Get out of the way, Barney, I'm going to give him all six chambers.'

'No,' said Barney quietly.

'Why?' demanded Curtiss, trying to push past Custer.

'Because I don't believe that he harmed Victoria,' replied Barney. 'That's sufficient reason for waiting until we know the truth. Then I won't stand for the killing of an unconscious man anyway.'

'He's nothing but a beast – a mad dog,' insisted Curtiss. 'He should be killed for what he is. I'd never have thought to see you defending the man who killed your sister – God alone knows what worse crime he committed before he killed her.'

'Don't be a fool, Curtiss,' snapped Barney. 'We don't even know that Victoria's dead. The chances are that this man has been helpless from fever for a long time. There's a wound in his head that was probably made by your shot last night. If he recovers from that he may be able to throw some light on Victoria's disappearance. If it develops that he has harmed her I'm the one to demand an accounting – not you; but as I said before I do not believe that this man would have harmed a hair of my sister's head.'

'What do you know about him?' demanded Curtiss.

'I never saw him before,' replied Barney. 'I don't know who he is or where he came from; but I know – well, never mind what I know, except that there isn't anybody going to kill him, other than Barney Custer.'

'Custer's right,' broke in Brown. 'It would be murder to kill this fellow in cold blood. You have jumped to the conclusion, Curtiss, that Miss Custer is dead. If we let you kill this man we might be destroying our best chance to locate and rescue her.'

As they talked the gaunt figure of the wolfhound, Terkoz, crept into the cave. He had not been killed by the Arab's blow, and a liberal dose of cold water poured over his head had helped to hasten returning consciousness. He nosed, whining, about the cavern as though in search of Victoria. The men watched him in silence after Brown had said: 'If this man harmed Miss Custer and laid out Terkoz the beast'll be keen for revenge. Watch him, and if Curtiss is right there won't any of us have to avenge your sister – Terkoz'll take care of that. I know him.'

'We'll leave it to Terkoz,' said Barney confidently.

After the animal had made the complete rounds of the cave, sniffing at every crack and crevice, he came to each of the watching men, nosing them carefully. Then he walked directly to the side of the unconscious Nu, licked his cheek, and lying down beside him rested his head upon the man's breast so that his fierce, wolfish eyes were pointed straight and watchful at the group of men opposite him.

'There,' said Barney, leaning down and stroking the beast's head.

The hound whined up into his face; but when Curtiss approached he rose, bristling, and standing across the body of Nu growled ominously at him.

'You'd better keep away from him, Curtiss,' warned Brown. 'He always has had a strange way with him in his likes and dislikes, and he's a mighty ugly customer to deal with when he's crossed. He's killed one man already – a big Wamboli spearman who was stalking Greystoke up in the north country last fall. Let's see if he's got it in for the rest of us;' but one by one Terkoz suffered the others to approach Nu – only Curtiss seemed to rouse his savage, protective instinct.

As they discussed their plans for the immediate future Nu opened his eyes with a return of consciousness. At sight of the strange figures about him he sat up and reached for his spear; but Barney had the foresight to remove this weapon as well as the man's knife and hatchet from his reach.

As the cave man came to a sitting posture Barney laid a hand upon his shoulder. 'We shall not harm you,' he said; 'if you will tell us what has become of my sister,' and then placing his lips close to the other's ear he whispered: 'Where is Nat-ul?'

Nu understood but the single word, Nat-ul; but the friendly tone and the hand upon his shoulder convinced him that this man was no enemy. He shook his head negatively. 'Nu does not understand the stranger's tongue,' he said. And then he asked the same question as had Barney: 'Where is Nat-ul?' But the American could translate only the name, yet it told him that here indeed was the dream-man of his sister.

When it became quite evident that the man could not understand anything that they said to him, and that he was in no condition to march, it was decided to send him back to the ranch by some of the native carriers that accompanied the searching party, while the others continued the search for the missing girl.

Terkoz suffered them to lift Nu in their arms and carry him outside where he was transferred to a rude litter constructed with a saddle blanket and two spears belonging to the Waziri hunters who had accompanied them.

Barney felt that this man might prove the key to the solution of Victoria's whereabouts, and so for fear that he might attempt to escape he decided to accompany him personally, knowing that the search for his sister would proceed as thoroughly without him as with. In the meantime he might be working out some plan whereby he could communicate with the stranger.

And so they set out for the ranch. Four half-naked blacks

bore the rude stretcher. Upon one side walked Terkoz, the wolfhound, and upon the other, Barney Custer. Four Waziri warriors accompanied them.

CHAPTER NINE

NU GOES TO FIND NAT-UL

Nu, weak and sick, was indifferent to his fate. If he had been captured by enemies, well and good. He knew what to expect – either slavery or death, for that was the way of men as Nu knew them. If slavery, there was always the chance to escape. If death, he would at least no longer suffer from loneliness in a strange world far from his own people and his matchless Nat-ul; whom he only saw now in his dreams.

He wondered what this strangely garbed stranger knew of Nat-ul. The man had most certainly spoken her name. Could it be possible that she, too, was a prisoner among these people? He had most certainly seen her in the garden before the strange cave where he had slain the diminutive Zor that had been about to devour her. That was no dream, he was positive, and so she must indeed be a prisoner.

As he recalled the lion he half smiled. What a runt of a beast it had been indeed! Why old Zor who hunted in the forest of the ape-people and dwelt in the caves upon the hither slopes of the Barren Hills would have snapped that fellow up in two bits. And Oo! A sneeze from Oo would have sent him scurrying into the Dark Swamp where Oo could not venture because of his great weight. It was an odd world in which Nu found himself. The country seemed almost barren to him, and yet he was in the heart of tropical Africa. The creatures seemed small and insignificant – yet the lion he had killed was one of the largest that Brown or Greystoke had ever seen – and he shivered, even in the heat of the equatorial sun.

How he longed for the world of his birth, with its mighty

beasts, its gigantic vegetation, and its hot, humid atmosphere through which its great, blurred sun appeared grotesquely large and close at hand!

For a week they doctored Nu at the bungalow of the Greystokes. There were times when they despaired of his life, for the bullet wound that creased his temple clear to the skull had become infected; but at last he commenced to mend, and after that his recovery was rapid, for his consituation was that of untainted physical perfection.

The several searching parties returned one by one without a clue to the whereabouts of Victoria Custer. Barney knew that all was being done that could be done by his friends; but he clung tenaciously to the belief that the solution to the baffling mystery lay locked in the breast of the strange giant who was convalescing upon the cot that had been set up for him in Barney's own room, for such had been the young American's wish. Curtiss had been relegated to other apartments, and Barney stuck close to the bedside of his patient day and night.

His principal reasons for so doing were his wish to prevent the man's escape, and his desire to open some method of communication with the stranger as rapidly as possible. Already the wounded man had learned to make known his simpler wants in English, and the ease with which he mastered whatever Barney attempted to teach him assured the American of the early success of his venture in this direction.

Curtiss continued to view the stranger with suspicion and ill disguised hostility. He was positive that the man had murdered Victoria Custer, and failing to persuade the others that they should take justice into their own hands and execute the prisoner forthwith, he now insisted that he be taken to the nearest point at which civilization had established the machinery of law and turned over to the authorities.

Barney, on the other hand, was just as firm in his determination to wait until the man had gained a sufficient command of English to enable them to give him a fair hearing, and then be governed accordingly. He could not forget that there had existed some strange and inexplicable bond between this handsome giant and his sister, nor that unquestionably the man had saved her life when 'old Raffles' had sprung upon her. Barney had loved, and lost because he had loved a girl beyond his reach and so his sympathies went out to this man who, he was confident, loved his sister. Uncanny as her dreams had been, Barney was forced to admit that there had been more to them than either Victoria or he had imagined, and now he felt that for Victoria's sake he should champion her dream-man in her absence.

One of the first things that Barney tried to impress upon the man was that he was a prisoner, and lest he should escape by night when Barney slept Greystoke set Terkoz to watch over him. But Nu did not seem inclined to wish to escape. His one desire apparently was to master the strange tongue of his captors. For two weeks after he was able to quit his bed he devoted his time to learning English. He had the freedom of the ranch, coming and going as he pleased, but his weapons were kept from him, hidden in Lord Greystoke's study, and Barney, sometimes with others of the household, always accompanied him.

Nu was waiting for Nat-ul. He was sure that she would come back again to this cave that his new acquaintances called a bungalow. Barney was waiting for the man to mention his sister. One day Curtiss came upon Nu sitting upon the veranda. Terkoz lay at his feet. Nu was clothed in khaki – an old suit of Greystoke's being the largest that could be found upon the place, and that was none too large. As Curtiss approached, the wolfhound turned his wicked little eyes upon him, without moving his head from where it lay stretched upon his forepaws, and growled. Nu extended a booted foot across the beast's neck to hold him in check.

The hound's show of hostility angered Curtiss. He hated the brute, and he hated Nu as cordially – just why, he did not know, for it seemed that his hatred of the stranger was a thing apart from his righteous anger in his belief that the man had guilty knowledge of the fate of Victoria Custer. He halted in front of the cave man.

'I want to ask you a question,' he said coldly. 'I have been wanting to do so for a long time; but there has always been someone else around.'

Nu nodded. 'What can Nu tell you?' he asked.

'You can tell me where Miss Custer is,' replied Curtiss.

'Miss Custer? I do not know what you mean. I never heard of Miss Custer.'

'You lie!' cried Curtiss, losing control of himself. 'Her jacket was found beneath your head in that foul den of yours.'

Nu came slowly to his feet.

'What does "lie" mean?' he asked. 'I do not understand all that people say to me, yet; but I can translate much from the manner and tone of the saying, and I do not like your tone, Curtiss.'

'Answer my question,' cried Curtiss. 'Where is Victoria Custer? And when you speak to me remember that I'm *Mr* Curtiss – you damned white nigger.'

'What does "lie" mean?' persisted Nu. 'And what is a "nigger"? And why should I call you mister? I do not like the sound of your voice, Curtiss.'

It was at this moment that Barney appeared. A single glance at the attitude of the two men warned him that he was barely in time to avert a tragedy. The black haired giant stood with the bristling wolfhound at his side. The attitude of the man resembled nothing more closely than that of a big, black panther tensed for a spring. Curtiss's hand was reaching for the butt of the gun at his hip. Barney stepped between them.

'What is the meaning of this, Curtiss?' he asked sharply. Curtiss had been a warm friend for years – a friend of civilization, and luxury and ease. He had known Curtiss under conditions which gave Curtiss everything that Curtiss wished, and Curtiss had seemed a fine fellow, but lately, since Curtiss had been crossed and disappointed, he had found sides to the man's character that had never before presented themselves. His narrow and unreasoning hatred for the half savage white man had caused the first doubts in Barney's mind as to the breadth of his friend's character. And then – most unpardonable of sins – Curtiss had grumbled at the hardships of the field while the searching parties had been out. Butzow had told Barney of it, and of how Curtiss had shirked much of the work which the other white men had assumed when there had been a dearth of competent servants in the camp.

Curtiss made no reply to Barney's question. Instead he turned on his heel and walked away. Nu laid a hand upon the American's shoulder.

'What does "lie" mean, Custer?' he asked.

Barney tried to explain.

'I see,' said Nu. 'And what is a "nigger" and a "mister"?'

Again Barney did his best to explain.

'Who is Miss Custer?' Nu asked.

Barney looked at the man in surprise.

'Do you not know?' he asked.

'Why should I?'

'She is my sister,' said Barney, looking closely at the man.

'Your sister?' questioned Nu. 'I did not know you had a sister, Custer.'

'You did not know my sister, Nat-ul?' cried Barney.

'Nat-ul!' exclaimed the man. 'Nat-ul your sister?'

'Yes. I supposed that you knew it.'

'But you are not Aht, son of Tha,' said Nu, 'and Nat-ul had no other brother.'

'I am brother of the girl you saved from the lion in the garden yonder,' said Barney. 'Is it she you know as Nat-ul?'

'She was Nat-ul.'

'Where is she?' cried Barney.

'I do not know,' replied Nu. 'I thought that she was a prisoner among you and I have been waiting here quietly for her to be brought back.'

'You saw her last,' said Barney. The time had come to have it out with this man. 'You saw her last. She was in your cave in the mountain. We found her jacket there, and beside the spring this dog lay senseless. What became of her?'

Nu stood with an expression of dull incomprehension upon his fine features. It was as though he had received a stunning blow.

'She was there?' he said at last in a low voice. 'She was there in my cave and I thought it was but a dream. She has gone away, and for many days I have remained here doing nothing while she roams amidst the dangers of the forest alone and unprotected. Unless,' his tone became more hopeful, 'she has found her way back to our own people among the caves beside the Restless Sea. But how could she? Not even I, a man and a great hunter, can even guess in what direction lies the country of my father, Nu. Perhaps you can tell me?'

Barney shook his head. His disappointment was great. He had been sure that Nu could cast some light upon the whereabouts of Victoria. He wondered if the man was telling him the truth. Doubts began to assail him. It seemed scarce credible that Victoria could have been in the fellow's lair without his knowing of her presence. That she had been there there seemed little or no doubt. The only other explanation was that Nu had, as Curtiss had suggested, stolen her from the vicinity of the bungalow, killed her, and taken his spear and her coat back to his cave with him; but that did not account for the presence of the hound or the beast's evident loyalty to the man.

Nu had turned from the veranda and entered the bungalow. Barney followed him. The cave man was hunting about the house for something.

'What are you looking for?' asked the American.

'My spear,' replied Nu.

'What do you want of it?'

'I'm going to find Nat-ul.'

Barney laid a hand upon the other's arm.

'No,' he said, 'you are not going away from here until we find my sister – you are a prisoner. Do you understand?'

The cave man drew himself to his full height. There was a sneer upon his lip. 'Who can prevent me?'

Barney drew his revolver. 'This,' he said.

For a moment the man seemed plunged in thought. He looked at the menacing gun, and then off through the open windows toward the distant hills.

'I can wait, for her sake,' he said.

'Don't make any attempt to escape,' warned Barney. 'You will be watched carefully. Terkoz will give the alarm even if he should be unable to stop you, though as a matter of fact he can stop you easily enough. Were I you I should hate to be stopped by Terkoz – he is as savage as a lion when aroused, and almost as formidable.'

Barney did not see the smile that touched the cave man's lips at this for he had turned away to resume his chair upon the veranda. Later Barney told the others that Nu seemed to realize the futility of attempting to get away, but that night he locked their door securely, placed the key under his pillow and drew his cot beneath the double windows of their room. It would take a mighty stealthy cat, thought he, to leave the apartment without arousing him, even were Terkoz not stretched beside the prisoner's cot.

About midnight the cave man opened his eyes. The regular breathing of the American attested the soundness of his slumber. Nu extended a hand toward the sleeping Terkoz, at the same time making a low, purring sound with his lips. The beast raised his head.

'Sh-h!' whispered Nu. Then he rose to a sitting posture, and very carefully put his feet to the floor. Stooping he lifted the heavy wolfhound in his arms. The only sign the animal made was to raise his muzzle to the man's face and lick his cheek. Nu smiled. He recalled Custer's words: 'Terkoz will give the alarm even if he should be unable to stop you.'

The troglodyte approached the cot on which Barney lay in peaceful slumber. He rested one hand upon the sill of the open window, leaning across the sleeper. Without a sound he vaulted over the cot, through the window and alighted noiselessly upon the veranda without. In the garden he deposited Terkoz, telling him to wait there, then he returned to the living room of the bungalow to fetch his spear, his hatchet and his knife. A moment later the figures of a naked man and gaunt wolfhound swung away beneath the tropic moon across the rolling plain toward the mountains to the south.

CHAPTER TEN

ON THE TRAIL

It was daylight when Barney Custer awoke. His first thought was for his prisoner, and when his eyes fell upon the empty cot across the room the American came to the center of the floor with a single bound. Clad in his pajamas he ran out into the living room and gave the alarm. In another moment the search was on, but no sign of the cave man was to be found, nor of the guardian Terkoz.

'He must have killed the dog,' insisted Greystoke; but they failed to find the beast's body, for the excellent reason that at that very moment Terkoz, bristling with anger, was nosing about the spot where, nearly a month before, he had been struck down by the Arab, as he had sought to protect the girl to whom he had attached himself.

As he searched the spot his equally savage companion hastened to the cave further up the mountainside, and with his knife unearthed the head of Oo which he had buried there in the soft earth of a crevice within the lair. The trophy was now in a rather sad state of putrefaction, and Nu felt that he must forego the pleasure of laying it intact at the feet of his future mate; but the great saber-teeth were there and the skull. He removed the former, fastening them to his gee-string and laid the balance of the head outside the cave where vultures might strip it clean of flesh against Nu's return, for he did not wish to be burdened with it during his search for Nat-ul.

A deep bay from Terkoz presently announced the finding of the trail and at the signal Nu leaped down the mountainside where the impatient beast awaited him. A moment later the two savage trailers were speeding away upon the spoor of the Arab slave and ivory raiders. Though the trail was old it still was sufficiently plain for these two. The hound's scent was but a trifle more acute than his human companion's, but the man depended almost solely upon the tell-tale evidences which his eyes could apprehend, leaving the scent-spoor to the beast, for thus it had been his custom to hunt with the savage wolfish progenitors of Terkoz a hundred thousand years before.

They moved silently and swiftly through the jungle, across valleys, over winding hill-trails, wherever the broad path of the caravan led. In a day they covered as much ground as the caravan had covered in a week. By night they slept at the foot of some great tree, the man and beast curled up together; or crawled within dark caves when the way led through the mountains; or, when Zor, the lion, was abroad the man would build a rude platform high among the branches of a tree that he and the hound might sleep in peace throughout the night.

Nu saw strange sights that filled him with wonder and sealed his belief that he had been miraculously transferred to another world. There were villages of black men, some of which gave evidence of recent conflict. Burned huts, and mutilated corpses were all that remained of many, and in others only a few old men and women were to be seen.

He also passed herds of giraffe – a beast that had been unknown in his own world, and many elephant which reminded him of Gluh, the mammoth. But all these beasts were smaller than those he had known in his other life, nor nearly so ferocious. Why, he could scarce recall a beast of any description that did not rush into a death struggle with the first member of another species which it came upon – provided, of course, that it stood the slightest show of despatching its antagonist. Of course there had been the smaller and more timid animals whose entire existence had consisted in snatching what food they could as they fled through the savage days and awful nights of that fierce age in the perpetual effort to escape or elude the countless myriads of huge carnivora and bellicose ruminants whose trails formed a mighty network from pole to pole.

So to Nu the jungles of Africa seemed silent and deserted places. The beasts, even the more savage of them, seldom attacked except in hunger or the protection of their young. Why, he had passed within a dozen paces of a great herd of these diminutive, hairless mammoths and they had but raised their little, pig eyes and glanced at him, as they flapped their great ears back and forth against the annoying flies and browsed upon the branches of young trees.

The ape-people seemed frightened out of their wits at his approach, and he had even seen the tawny bodies of lions pass within a stone's throw of him without charging. It was amazing. Life in such a world would scarce be worth the living. It made him lonelier than ever to feel that he could travel for miles without encountering a single danger.

Far behind him along the trail of the Arabs came a dozen white men and half a hundred savage Waziri warriors. Not an hour after Barney Custer discovered Nu's absence a native runner had come hurrying in from the north to beg Lord Greystoke's help in pursuing and punishing a band of Arab slave and ivory raiders who were laying waste the villages, murdering the old men and the children and carrying the young men and women into slavery.

While Greystoke was questioning the fellow he let drop the fact that among the other prisoners of the Arabs was a young white woman. Instantly commotion reigned upon the Greystoke ranch. White men were jumping into field khaki, looking to firearms and ammunition lest their black body servants should have neglected some essential. Stable boys were saddling the horses, and the sleek, ebon warriors of Uziri were greasing their black hides, adjusting barbaric war bonnets, streaking faces, breasts, limbs and bellies with ocher, vermillion or ghastly bluish white, and looking to slim shield, poisoned arrow and formidable war spear.

For a time the fugitive was forgotten, but as the march proceeded they came upon certain reminders that recalled him to their thoughts and indicated that he was far in advance of them upon the trail of the Arabs. The first sign of him was the carcass of a bull buffalo. Straight through the heart was the great hole that they now knew was made by the passage of the ancient, stone tipped spear. Strips had been knife cut from the sides, and the belly was torn as though by a wild beast. Brown stooped to examine the ground about the bull. When he straightened up he looked at Greystoke and laughed.

'Didn't I understand you to say that he must have killed the dog?' he asked. 'Look here – they ate side by side from the body of their kill.'

CHAPTER ELEVEN

THE ABDUCTION

For three weeks now Victoria Custer had been a prisoner of Sheik Ibn Aswad, but other than the ordinary hardships of African travel she had experienced nothing of which she might complain. She had even been permitted to ride upon one of the few donkeys that still survived, and her food was as good as that of Ibn Aswad himself, for the canny old sheik knew that the better the condition of his prisoner the better the price she would bring at the court of the sultan of Fulad.

Abul Mukarram, Ibn Aswad's right hand man, a swaggering young Arab from the rim of the Sahara, had cast covetous eyes upon the beautiful prisoner, but the old sheik delivered himself of a peremptory no when his lieutenant broached a proposal to him. Then Abul Mukarram, balked in his passing desire found the thing growing upon him until the idea of possessing the girl became a veritable obsession with him.

Victoria, forced to it by necessity, had picked up enough of the language of the sons of the desert to be able to converse with them, and Abul Mukarram often rode at her side feasting his eyes upon her face and figure the while he attempted to ingratiate himself into her esteem by accounts of his prowess; but when at last he spoke of love the girl turned her flushed and angry face away from him, and reining in her donkey refused to ride further beside him.

Ibn Aswad from afar witnessed the altercation, and when

he rode to Victoria's side and learned the truth of the matter he berated Abul Mukarram roundly, ordered him to the rear of the column and placed another Arab over the prisoner. Thereafter the venomous looks which the discredited Abul cast upon Victoria oftentimes caused her to shudder inwardly, for she knew that she had made a cruel and implacable enemy of the man.

Ibn Aswad had given her but a hint of the fate which awaited her, yet it had been sufficient to warn her that death were better than the thing she was being dragged through the jungles to suffer. Every waking minute her mind was occupied with plans for escape, yet not one presented itself which did not offer insuperable obstacles.

Even had she been able to leave the camp undetected how long could she hope to survive in the savage jungle? And should, by some miracle, her life be spared even for months, of what avail would that be, for she could no more have retraced her way to Lord Greystoke's ranch than she could have laid a true course upon the trackless ocean.

The horrors of the march that passed daily in hideous review before her left her sick and disgusted. The cruelly beaten slaves who carried the great burdens of ivory, tents and provisions brought tears to her eyes. The brutal massacres that followed the forcible entrance into each succeeding village wrung her heart and aroused her shame for those beasts in human form who urged on their savage and cowardly Manyuema cannibals to commit nameless excesses against the cowering prisoners that fell into their hands.

But at last they came to a village where victory failed to rush forward and fall into their arms. Instead they were met with sullen resistance. Ferocious, painted devils fought them stubbornly every inch of the way, until Ibn Aswad decided to make a detour and pass around the village rather than sacrifice more of his followers.

In the confusion of the fight, and the near-retreat which followed it, Abul Mukarram found the opportunity he had been awaiting. The prisoners, including the white girl, were being pushed ahead of the retreating raiders, while the

Arabs and Manyuema brought up the rear, fighting off the pursuing savages.

Now Abul Mukarram knew a way to the northland that two might traverse with ease, and over which one could fairly fly; but which was impossible for a slave caravan because it passed through the territory of the English. If the girl would accompany him willingly, well and good – if not, then he would go alone but not before he had committed upon her the revenge he had planned. He left the firing line, therefore, and pushed his way through the terror stricken slaves to the side of the Arab who guarded Victoria Custer.

'Go back to Ibn Aswad,' he said to the Arab. 'He desires your presence.'

The other looked at him closely for a moment. 'You lie, Abul Mukarram,' he said at last. 'Ibn Aswad commanded me particularly against permitting you to be alone with the girl. Go to!'

'Fool!' muttered Abul Mukarram, and with the word he pulled the trigger of the long gun that rested across the pummel of his saddle with its muzzle scarce a foot from the stomach of the other Arab. With a single shriek the man lunged from his donkey.

'Come!' cried Abul Mukarram, seizing the bridle of Victoria's beast and turning into the jungle to the west.

The girl tried to slip from her saddle, but a strong arm went about her waist and held her firm as the two donkeys forged, shoulder to shoulder through the tangled mass of creepers which all but blocked their way. Once Victoria screamed for help, but the savage war cries of the natives drowned her voice. Fifteen minutes later the two came out upon the trail again that they had followed when they approached the village and soon the sounds of the conflict behind them grew fainter and fainter until they were lost entirely in the distance.

Victoria Custer's mind was working rapidly, casting about for some means of escape from the silent figure at her side. A revolver or even a knife would have solved her difficulty, but she had neither. Had she, the life of Abul Mukarram would have been worth but little, for the girl was beside herself with hopeless horror of the fate that now loomed so close at hand. The thought that she had not even the means to take her own life left her numb and cold. There was but one way; to battle with tooth and nail until, in anger, the man himself should kill her; yet until the last moment she might hope against hope for the succor which she knew in her heart of hearts it was impossible to receive.

For the better part of two hours Abul Mukarram kept on away from the master he had robbed. He spoke but little, and when he did it was in the tone of the master to his slave. Near noon they left the jungle and came out into a higher country where the space between the trees was greater, and there was little or no underbrush. Traveling was much easier here and they made better time. They were still retracing the trail along which the caravan had traveled. It would be some time during the next morning that they would turn north again upon a new trail.

Beside a stream Abul Mukarram halted. He tethered the donkeys, and then turned toward the girl. 'Come,' he said, and laid his hand upon her.

CHAPTER TWELVE

THE CAVE MAN FINDS HIS MATE

Each day Nu realized that he was gaining rapidly upon those with whom Nat-ul traveled. The experiences of his other life assured him that she must be a prisoner, yet at the same time he realized that such might not be the case at all, for had he not thought her a prisoner among the others who had held him prisoners, only to learn that one of them claimed her as a sister. It all seemed very strange to Nu. It was quite beyond him. Nat-ul could not be the sister of Custer, and yet he had seen her apparently happy and contented in the society of these strangers, and Custer unquestionably appeared to feel for her the solicitude of a brother. Curtiss, it was evident, loved Nat-ul – that much he had gleaned from conversations he had overheard between him and Custer. How the man could have become so well acquainted with Nat-ul between the two days that had elapsed since Nu had set forth from the caves beside the Restless Sea to hunt down Oo and the morning that he had awakened following the mighty shaking of the world was quite as much a mystery as was the remarkable changes that had taken place in the aspect of the world during the same brief period. Nu had given much thought to those miraculous happenings, with the result that he had about convinced himself that he must have slept much longer than he had believed; but that a hundred thousand years had rolled their slow and weary progress above his unconscious head could not, of course, have occurred to him even as the remotest of possibilities.

He had also weighed the sneering words of Curtiss and with them the attitude of the strangers with whom he had been thrown. He had quickly appreciated the fact that their manners and customs were as far removed from his as they were from those of the beasts of the jungle. He had seen that his own ways were more in accordance with the ways of the black and half naked natives whom the whites looked upon as so much their inferiors that they would not even eat at the same table with them.

He had noted the fact that the blacks treated the other whites with a marked respect which they did not extend to Nu, and being no fool Nu had come to the conclusion that the whites themselves looked upon him as an inferior, even before Curtiss's words convinced him of the truth of his suspicions. Evidently, though his skin was white, he was in some subtile way different from the other whites. Possibly it was in the matter of raiment. He had tried to wear the strange body coverings they had given him, but they were cumbersome and uncomfortable and though he was seldom warm enough now he had nevertheless been glad when the opportunity came to discard the hampering and unaccustomed clothing.

These thoughts suggested the possibility that if Nat-ul had found recognition among the strangers upon an equal footing with them that she, too, might have those attributes of superiority which the strangers claimed, and if such was the fact it became evident that she would consider Nu from the viewpoint of her new friends – as an inferior.

Such reveries made Nu very sad, for he loved Nat-ul just as you or I would love – just as normal white men have always loved – with a devotion that placed the object of his affection upon a pedestal before which he was happy to bow down and worship. His passion was not of the brute type of the inferior races which oftentimes solemnizes the marriage ceremony with a cudgel and ever places the woman in the position of an inferior and a chattel.

Even as Nu pondered the puzzling questions which confronted him his eyes and ears were alert as he sped along the now fresh trail of the caravan. Every indication pointed the recent passing of many men, and the troglodyte was positive that he could be but a few hours behind his quarry.

A few miles east of him the rescue party from the Greystoke ranch were pushing rapidly ahead upon a different trail with a view to heading off the Arabs. Ibn Aswad had taken a circuitous route in order that he might pass around the country of the Waziri, and with his slow moving slave caravan he had now reached a point but a few days' journey in a direct line from the ranch. The lightly equipped pursuers having knowledge of the route taken by the Arabs from the messenger who had come to seek their assistance had not been compelled to follow the spoor of their quarry but instead had marched straight across country in a direct line for a point which they believed would bring them ahead of the caravan.

Thus it was that Nu and Terkoz, and the party of whites and Waziri from the ranch were closing in upon Ibn Aswad from opposite directions simultaneously; but Nu was not destined to follow the trail of the raiders to where they were still engaged in repelling the savage attacks of the fierce Wamboli, for as he trotted along with the dog at his side his quick eyes detected that which the hound, with all his wondrous instinctive powers, would have passed by, unnoticing – the well-marked prints of the hoofs of two donkeys that had come back along the trail since the caravan had passed.

That they were donkeys belonging to the Arabs was evident to Nu through his familiarity with the distinctive hoof prints of each, which during the past three days had become as well known to him as his mother's face had been. But what were they doing retracing the way they had but just covered! Nu halted and raised his head to sniff the air and listen intently for the faintest sound from the direction in which the beasts had gone when they left the old trail at the point where he had discovered their spoor.

But the wind was blowing from the opposite direction, so there was no chance that Nu could scent them. He was in doubt as to whether he should leave the trail of the main body and follow these two, or continue on his way. From the manner of their passing – side by side – he was convinced that each carried a rider, since otherwise they would have gone in single file after the manner of beasts moving along a none too wide trail; but there was nothing to indicate that either rider was Nat-ul.

For an instant he hesitated, and then his judgment told him to keep on after the main body, for if Nat-ul was a prisoner she would be with the larger force – not riding in the opposite direction with a single guard. Even as he turned to take up the pursuit again there came faintly to his ears from the jungle at his left the sound of a human voice – it was a woman's, raised in frightened protest.

Like a deer Nu turned and leaped in the direction of that familiar voice. The fleet wolfhound was put to it to keep pace with the agile cave man, for Nu had left the earth and taken to the branches of the trees where no underbrush retarded his swift flight. From tree to tree he leaped or swung, sometimes hurling his body twenty feet through the air from one jungle giant to another. Below him raced the panting Terkoz, red tongue lolling from his foam flecked mouth; but with all their speed the two moved with the noiselessness of shadowy ghosts.

At the edge of the jungle Nu came upon a park-like forest, and well into this he saw a white robed Arab forcing a woman slowly backward across his knee. One sinewy, brown hand clutched her throat, the other was raised to strike her in the face.

Nu saw that he could not reach the man in time to prevent the blow, but he might distract his attention for the moment that would be required for him to reach his side. From his throat there rose the savage war cry of his long dead people – a cry that brought a hundred jungle creatures to their feet trembling in fear or in rage according to their kind. And it brought Abul Mukarram upstanding too, for in all his life he had never heard the like of that blood-freezing challenge.

At the sight which met his eyes he dropped the girl and darted toward his donkey where hung his long barreled rifle in its boot. Victoria Custer looked, too, and what she saw brought unutterable relief and happiness to her. Then the Arab had turned with leveled gun just as the cave man leaped upon him. There was the report of the firearm ere it was wrenched from Abul Mukarram's grasp and hurled to one side, but the bullet went wide of its mark and the next instant the girl saw the two men locked in what she knew was a death struggle. The Arab struck mighty blows at the head and face of his antagonist, while the cave man, the great muscles rolling beneath his smooth hide, sought for a hold upon the other's throat.

About the two the vicious wolfhound slunk growling with bristling hair, waiting for an opportunity to rush in upon the white robed antagonist of his master. Victoria Custer, her clenched fists tight pressed against her bosom, watched the two men who battled for her. She saw the handsome black head of her savage man bend lower and lower toward the throat of his foeman, and when the strong, white teeth buried themselves in the jugular of the other it was with no sickening qualm of nausea that the girl witnessed the bestial act.

She heard the half wolfish growl of Nu as he tasted the hot, red blood of his enemy. She saw the strong jaws tear and rend the soft flesh of the Arab's throat. She saw the powerful hands bend back the head of the doomed Abul Mukarram. She saw her ferocious mate shake the man as a terrier shakes a rat, and her heart swelled in fierce primitive pride at the prowess of her man.

No longer did Victoria Custer exist. It was Nat-ul, the savage maiden of the Niocene who, as Nu threw the lifeless corpse of his kill to one side, and opened his arms, flung herself into his embrace. It was Nat-ul, daughter of Tha – Nat-ul of the tribe of Nu that dwelt beyond the Barren Cliffs beside the Restless Sea who threw her arms about her lord and master's neck and drew his mouth down to her hot lips.

It was Nat-ul of the first born who watched Nu and the fierce wolfhound circle about the corpse of the dead Arab. The cave man, moving in the graceful, savage steps of the death dance of his tribe, now bent half over, now leaping high in air, throwing his stone-tipped spear aloft, chanting the weird victory song of a dead and buried age, and beside him his equally savage mate squatted upon her haunches beating time with her slim, white hands.

When the dance was done Nu halted before Nat-ul. The girl rose, facing him and for a long minute the two stood in silence looking at one another. It was the first opportunity that either had had to study the features of the other since the strange miracle that had separated them. Nu found that some subtle change had taken place in his Nat-ul. It was she – of that there could be no doubt; but yet there was that about her which cast a spell of awe over him – she was infinitely finer and more wonderful than he ever had realized.

With the passing of the excitement of the battle and the dance the strange ecstasy which had held the girl in thrall passed slowly away. The rhythm of the dancing of the savage, black haired giant had touched some chord within her which awoke the long dormant instinct of the primordial. For the time she had been carried back a hundred thousand years to the childhood of the human race – she had not known for those brief instants Victoria Custer, or the twentieth century, or its civilization, for they were yet a thousand centuries in the future.

But now she commenced once more to look through the eyes of generations of culture and refinement. Before her she saw a savage, primitive man. In his eyes was the fire of a great love that would not for long be denied. About her she saw the wild, fierce forest and the cruel jungle, and behind all this, and beyond, her vision wandered to the world she had always known – the world of cities and homes and gentlefolk. She saw her father and her mother and her friends. What would they say?

Again she let her eyes rest upon the man. It was with difficulty that she restrained a mad desire to throw herself upon his broad breast and weep out her doubts and fears close to the beating of his great heart and in the safety of those mighty, protecting arms. But with the wish there arose again the question – what would they say? – held her trembling and frightened from him.

The man saw something of the girl's trouble in her eyes, but he partially misinterpreted it, for he read fear of himself where there was principally self-fear, and because of what he had heard Curtiss say he thought that he saw contempt too, for primitive people are infinitely more sensitive than their more sophisticated brothers.

'You do not love me, Nat-ul?' he asked. 'Have the strangers turned you against me? What one of them could have fetched you the head of Oo, the man hunter? See!' He tapped the two great tusks that hung from his loin cloth. 'Nu slew the mightiest of beasts for his Nat-ul – the head is buried in the cave of Oo – yet now that I come to take you as my mate I see fear in your eyes and something else which never was there before. What is it, Nat-ul – have the strangers stolen your love from Nu?'

The man spoke in a tongue so ancient that in all the world there lived no man who spoke or knew a word of it, yet to Victoria Custer it was as intelligible as her own English, nor did it seem strange to her that she answered Nu in his own language.

'My heart tells me that I am yours, Nu,' she said, 'but my judgment and my training warn me against the step that my heart prompts. I love you; but I could not be happy to wander, half naked, through the jungle for the balance of my life, and if I go with you now, even for a day, I may never return to my people. Nor would you be happy in the life that I lead – it would stifle and kill you. I think I see now something of the miracle that has overwhelmed us. To you it has been but a few days since you left your Nat-ul to hunt down the ferocious Oo; but in reality countless ages have rolled by. By some strange freak of fate you have remained unchanged during all these ages until now you step forth from your long sleep an unspoiled cave man of the stone age into the midst of the twentieth century, while I, doubtless, have been born and reborn a thousand times, merging from one incarnation to another until in this we are again united. Had you, too, died and been born again during all these weary years no gap of ages would intervene between us now and we should meet again upon a common footing as do other souls, and mate and die to be born again to a new mating and a new life with its inevitable death. But you have defied the laws of life and death – you have refused to die and now that we meet again at last a hundred thousand years lie between us – an unbridgable gulf across which I may not return and over which you may not come other than by the same route which I have followed – through death and a new life thereafter.'

Much that the girl said was beyond Nu's comprehension, and the most of it without the scope of his primitive language so that she had been forced to draw liberally upon her twentieth century English to fill in the gaps, yet Nu had caught the idea in a vague sort of way – at least that his Nat-ul was far removed from him because of a great lapse of time that had occurred while he slept in the cave of Oo, and that through his own death alone could he span the gulf between them and claim her as his mate.

He placed the butt of his spear upon the ground, resting the stone tip against his heart. 'I go, Nat-ul,' he said simply, 'that I may return again as you would have me – no longer the "white nigger" that Curtiss says I am.'

The girl and the man were so occupied and engrossed with their own tragedy that they did not note the restless pacing of Terkoz, the wolfhound, or hear the ominous growls that rumbled from his savage throat as he looked toward the jungle behind them.

CHAPTER THIRTEEN

INTO THE JUNGLE

The searching party from the Greystoke ranch had come upon Ibn Aswad so unexpectedly that not a shot had been exchanged between the two parties. The Arabs pressed from behind by the savage Wamboli warriors had literally run into the arms of the whites and the Waziri.

When Greystoke demanded that the white girl be turned over to him at once Ibn Aswad smote his breast and swore that there had been no white girl with them, but one of the slaves told a different story to a Waziri, and when the whites found that Victoria had been stolen from Ibn Aswad by one of the sheik's lieutenants only a few hours before they hastened to scour the jungle in search of her.

To facilitate their movements and insure covering as wide a territory as possible each of the whites took a few Waziri and spreading out in a far flung skirmish line beat the jungle in the direction toward which the slave had told them Abul Mukarram had ridden.

To comb the jungle finely each white spread his Waziri upon either side of him and thus they advanced, seldom in sight of one another; but always within hailing distance. And so it happened that chance brought William Curtiss, unseen, to the edge of the jungle beside the park-like forest beneath the giant trees of which he saw a tableau that brought him to a sudden halt.

There was the girl he loved and sought, apparently unharmed; and two donkeys; and the dead body of an Arab; and the great wolfhound, looking toward his hiding place and growling menacingly; and before the girl the savage white man stood. Curtiss was about to spring forward when he saw the man place the butt of his spear upon the ground and the point against his heart. The act and the expression upon the man's face proclaimed his intention, and so Curtiss drew back again waiting for the perpetration of the deed that he knew was coming. A smile of anticipation played about the American's lips.

Victoria Custer, too, guessed the thing that Nu contemplated. It was, in accordance with her own reasoning, the only logical thing for the man to do; but love is not logical, and when love saw and realized the imminence of its bereavement it cast logic to the winds, and with a little scream of terror the girl threw herself upon Nu of the Niocene, striking the spear from its goal.

'No! No!' she cried. 'You must not do it. I cannot let you go. I love you, Nu; oh, how I love you,' and as the strong arms infolded her once more she gave a happy sigh of content and let her head drop again upon the breast of him who had come back out of the ages to claim her.

The man put an arm about her waist, and together the two turned toward the west in the direction that Abul Mukarram had been fleeing; nor did either see the white faced, scowling man who leaped from the jungle behind them, and with leveled rifle took deliberate aim at the back of the black haired giant.

Nor did they see the swift spring of the wolfhound, nor the thing that followed there beneath the brooding silence of the savage jungle.

Ten minutes later Barney Custer broke through the tangled wall of verdure upon a sight that took his breath away – there stood the two patient donkeys, switching their tails and flapping their long ears; beside them lay the corpse of Abul Mukarram, and upon the edge of the jungle, at his feet, was stretched the dead body of William Curtiss, his breast and throat torn by savage fangs. Across the clearing a great, gaunt wolfhound halted in its retreat at the sound of Barney's approach. It bared its bloody fangs in an ominous growl of warning, and then turned and disappeared into the jungle.

Barney advanced and examined the soft ground about the donkeys and the body of the Arab. He saw the imprints of a man's naked feet, and the smaller impress of a woman's riding boot. He looked toward the jungle where Terkoz had disappeared.

What had his sister gone to within the somber, savage depths beyond? What would he bring her back to were he to follow after? He doubted that she would come without her dream-man. Where would she be happier with him – in the pitiless jungle which was the only world he knew, or in the still more pitiless haunts of civilized men?

PART TWO

CHAPTER ONE

AGAIN A WORLD UPHEAVAL

Victoria Custer was aware that Barney Custer, her brother, was forcing his way through the jungle behind them – that he was coming to take her away from Nu.

Many lifetimes of culture and refinement plead with her to relinquish her mad, idyllic purpose – to give up her savage man and return to the protection and comforts that her brother and civilization represented. But there was still another force at work, older by far then the brief span of cultivation that had marked the advancement of her more recent forebears – the countless ages of prehistoric savagery in which the mind and heart and soul of man were born – the countless awful ages that have left upon the soul and heart and mind of man an impress that will endure so long as man endures. From out of that black abyss before man had either mind or soul there still emanates the same mighty power that was his sole master then – instinct.

And it was instinct that drove Victoria Custer deeper into the jungle with her savage lover as she sensed the nearer approach of her brother – one of the two master instincts that have dominated and preserved life upon the face of the earth. Yet it was not without a struggle. She hesitated, half turning backward. Nu cast a questioning look upon her.

'They are coming, Nat-ul,' he said. 'Nu cannot fight these strange men who hurl lead with the thunders they have stolen from the skies. Come! We must hurry back to the cave of Oo, and on the morrow we shall go forth and search for the tribe of Nu, my father, that dwells beyond the Barren

Cliffs beside the Restless Sea. There, in our own world, we shall be happy.'

And yet the girl held back, afraid. Then the man gathered her in his mighty arms and ran on in the direction of the cave of Oo, the saber-toothed tiger. The girl did not even struggle to escape, instead she lay quietly, as over her fell a sensation of peace and happiness, as though after a long absence, she was being borne home. And at their heels trotted Terkoz, the wolfhound.

Sometimes Nu took to the lower branches of the trees, for in her own age his race had been semiarboreal. Here he traveled with the ease and agility of a squirrel, though oftentimes the modern woman that still lived in the breast of Victoria Custer quailed at the dizzy leaps, and the swaying, perilous trail. Yet, as they fled, her fears were greatest now that they might be overtaken, and herself snatched back into the world of civilization where her Nu could never follow.

It was dusk of the third evening when they came again to the cave of Oo. Up the steep cliff side they clambered, hand in hand. Together they entered the dark and forbidding hole.

'Tomorrow,' said Nu, 'we will search for the caves of our people, and we shall find them.'

Darkness settled upon the jungle, the plain and the mountains. Nu and Nat-ul slept, for both were exhausted from the long days of flight.

And then there came, out of the bowels of the earth, a deep and ominous rumbling. The earth shook. The cliff rocked. Great masses of shattered rock shaken from its summit roared and tumbled down its face.

Nu sprang to his feet, only to be hurled immediately to the floor of the cave stunned and senseless. Within all was darkness. No light filtered through the opening. For minutes the frightful din endured, and with it the sickening tossing of the earth; but, at last, the rumblings ceased, the world sank back to rest, exhausted.

And Nu lay unconscious where he had fallen.

CHAPTER TWO

BACK TO THE STONE AGE

It was morning when Nat-ul awoke. The sun was streaming in across a wide sea to illumine the interior of the cave where she lay huddled in a great pile of soft, furry pelts. Near her lay a woman, older than herself, but still beautiful. In front of them, nearer the mouth of the cave, two men slept. One was Tha, her father, and the other her brother, Aht. The woman was Nat-ul's mother, Lu-tan. Now she, too, opened her eyes. She stretched, raising her bare, brown arms above her head, and half turning on her side toward Nat-ul – it was the luxurious movement of the she-tiger – the embodiment of perfect health and grace. Lu-tan smiled at her daughter, exposing a row of strong, white, even teeth. Nat-ul returned the smile.

'I am glad that it is light again,' said the girl. 'The shaking of the ground, yesterday, frightened me, so that I had the most terrible dreams all during the darkness – ugh!' and Nat-ul shuddered.

Tha opened his eyes and looked at the two women.

'I, too, dreamed,' he said. 'I dreamed that the earth shook again; the cliffs sank; and the Restless Sea rolled in upon them, drowning us all. This is no longer a good place to live. After we have eaten I shall go speak to Nu, telling him that we should seek other caves in a new country.'

Nat-ul rose and stepping between the two men came to the ledge before the entrance to the cave. Before her stretched a scene that was perfectly familiar and yet strangely new. Below her was an open patch at the foot of the cliff, all barren and boulder strewn except for a rude rectangle that had been cleared of rock and debris. Beyond lay a narrow strip of tangled tropical jungle. Enormous fern-like trees lifted their huge fronds a hundred feet into the air.

The sun was topping the horizon, coming out of a great sea that lay just beyond the jungle. And such a sun! It was dull red and swollen to an enormous size. The atmosphere was thick and hot – almost sticky. And the life! Such countless myriads of creatures teeming through the jungle, winging their way through the air, and blackening the surface of the sea!

Nat-ul knit her brows. She was trying to think – trying to recall something. Was it her dream that she attempted to visualize, or was this the dream? She shook herself. Then she glanced quickly down at her apparel. For an instant she seemed not to comprehend the meaning of her garmenture – the single red-doe skin, or the sandals of the thick hide of Ta, the woolly rhinoceros, held to her shapely feet by thin lacings of the rawhide of the great Bos. And yet, she quickly realized, she had always been clothed just thus – but, had she? The question puzzled her.

Mechanically her hand slipped to the back of her head above the nape of her neck. A look of puzzlement entered her eyes as her fingers fell upon the loose strands of her long hair that tumbled to her waist in the riotous and lovely confusion of early morning. What was it that her light touch missed? A barette? What could Nat-ul, child of the stone age, know of barettes?

Slowly her fingers felt about her head. When they came in contact with the broad fillet that bound her hair back from her forehead she smiled. This was the fillet that Nu, the son of Nu, had fashioned for her from a single gorgeous snake skin of black and red and yellow, split lengthwise and dried. It awoke her to a more vivid realization of the present. She turned and re-entered the cave. From a wooden peg driven into a hole in the wall she took a handful of brilliant feathers. These she stuck in the front of the fillet, where they nodded in a gay plume above her sweet face.

By this time Lu-tan, Tha, and Aht had risen. The older woman was busying herself with some dry tinder and a fire stick, just inside the entrance to the cave. Tha and Aht had stepped out upon the ledge, filling their lungs with the morning air. Nat-ul joined them. In her hand was a bladder. The three clambered down the face of the cliff.

Other men and women were emerging from other caves that pitted the rocky escarpment. They greeted the three with smiles and pleasant words, and upon every tongue was some comment upon the earthquake of the preceding night.

Tha and Aht went into the jungle toward the sea. Nat-ul stopped beside a little spring, that bubbled, clear and cold, at the foot of the cliff. Here were other girls with bladders which they were filling with water. There was Ra-el, daughter of Kor, who made the keenest spear tips and the best balanced. And there was Una, daughter of Nu, the chief, and sister of Nu, the son of Nu. And beside these were half a dozen others – all clean limbed, fine featured girls, straight as arrows, supple as panthers. They laughed and talked as they filled their bladders at the spring.

'Were you not frightened when the earth shook, Nat-ul?' asked Una.

'I was frightened,' replied Nat-ul – 'yes; but I was more frightened by the dream I had after the shaking had stopped.'

'What did you dream?' cried Ra-el, daughter of Kor – Kor who made the truest spear heads, with which a strong man could strike a flying reptile in mid-air.

'I dreamed that I was not Nat-ul,' replied the girl. 'I dreamed of a strange world and strange people. I was one of them. I was clothed in many garments that were not skin at all. I lived in a cave that was not a cave – it was built upon the ground of the stuff of which trees are made, only cut into thin slabs and fastened together. There were many caves in the one cave.

'There were men and women, and some of the men were *black*.'

'*Black!*' echoed the other girls.

'Yes, black,' insisted Nat-ul. 'And they alone were garbed something as are our men. The white men wore strange garments and things upon their heads, and had no beards. They carried short spears that spit smoke and great noise out upon their enemies and the wild beasts, and slew them at a great distance.'

'And was Nu, the son of Nu, there?' asked Ra-el, tittering behind her hand.

'He came and took me away,' replied Nat-ul, gravely. 'And at night the earth shook as we slept in the cave of Oo. And when I awoke I was here in the cave of Tha, my father.'

'Nu has not returned,' said Una.

Nat-ul looked at her enquiringly.

'Where did Nu, the son of Nu, go?' she asked.

'Who should know better than Nat-ul, daughter of Tha, that Nu, the son of Nu, went forth to slay Oo, the killer of men and mammoths, that he might lay Oo's head before the cave of Nat-ul?' she asked, in reply.

'He has not returned?' asked Nat-ul. 'He said that he would go but I thought that he joked, for one man alone may not slay Oo, the killer of men and of mammoths.' But she did not use the word 'mammoth', nor the word 'man'. Instead she spoke in a language that survives only among the apes of our day, if it survives at all, and among them only in crude and disjointed monosyllables. When she spoke of the mammoth she called him Gluh, and man was Pah. The tongue was low and liquid and entirely beautiful and enchanting, and she spoke, too, much with her eyes and with her graceful hands, as did her companions, for the tribe of Nu was not far removed from those earlier peoples, descended from the alalus who were speechless, and who preceded those who spoke by signs.

The girls, having filled the bladders with water, now returned to their respective caves. Nat-ul had scarce entered and hung up the bladder ere Tha and Aht returned – one with the carcass of an antelope, the other with an armful of fruits.

In the floor of the cave beside the fire a little hollow had been chipped from the living rock. Into this Nat-ul poured some water, while Lu-tan cut pieces of the antelope's flesh into small bits, dropping them into the water. Then she scooped a large pebble from the fire where it had been raised to a high temperature. This she dropped into the water with the meat. There was a great bubbling and sputtering, which was repeated as Lu-tan dropped one super-heated pebble after another into the water until the whole became a boiling cauldon. When the water continued to boil for a few moments after a pebble was thrown in Lu-tan eased her operation, sitting quietly with her family about the primitive stew for several minutes. Occasionally she would stick a finger into the water to test its temperature, and when at last she seemed satisfied she signalled Tha to eat.

The man plunged his stone knife into a piece of the half-cooked meat, withdrew it from the cauldron and tossed it upon the floor beside Lu-tan. A second piece was given to Nat-ul, a third to Aht, and the fourth Tha kept to himself. The four ate with a certain dignity. There was nothing bestial nor repulsive in their manners, and as they ate they talked and laughed among themselves – there seemed great good-fellowship in the cavehold of Tha.

Aht joked with Nat-ul about Nu, the son of Nu, telling her that doubtless a hyena had devoured the mighty hunter before ever he had had a chance to slay Oo. But Lu-tan came to her daugher's rescue, saying that it was more likely that Nu, the son of Nu, had discovered Oo and all his family and had remained to kill them all.

'I do not fear for Nu, because of Oo,' said Tha, presently. 'For Nu, the son of Nu, is as great a hunter as his father; but I shall be glad to see him safe again from all that might have befallen him when the earth rocked and the thunder came from below instead of from above. I shall be glad to have him return and take my daughter as his mate, whether he brings back the head of Oo or not.'

Nat-ul was silent, but she was worried, for all feared the power of the elements against which no man might survive in battle, no matter how brave he might be.

After breakfast Tha went, as he had said that he should, to the cave of Nu, the chief. There he found many of the older warriors and the young men. There were so many of them that there was not room within the cave and upon the narrow ledge without, so, at a word from Nu, they all descended to the little, roughly cleared rectangle at the base of the cliff. This place was where their councils were held and where the tribe congregated for feasts, or other purposes that called many together.

Nu sat at one end of the clearing upon a flat rock. About his shoulders fell the shaggy haired skin of a huge cave-bear. In the string that supported his lion cloth reposed a wooden handled stone axe and a stone knife. Upright in his hand, its butt between his feet, rose a tall, slim spear, stone tipped. His black hair was rudely cut into a shock. A fillet of tiger hide encircled his head, supporting a single long, straight feather. About his neck depended a string of long, sharp fangs and talons, and from cheek to heel his smooth, bronzed hide was marked with many scars inflicted by these same mementos when they had armed the mighty paws and jaws of the fierce denizens of that primeval world. He let the skin that covered him slip from his shoulders, for the morning was warm. In that hot and humid atmosphere there was seldom need for covering, but even then men were slaves to fashion. They were the trophies of their prowess, and bedecked their women similarly.

Tha, being second only to Nu, was the first among the warriors to speak. As speech was young and words comparatively few they must needs be supplemented with many signs and gestures. Oratory was, therefore, a strenuous business, and one which required a keen imagination, more than ordinary intelligence, and considerable histrionic ability. Because it was so difficult to convey one's ideas to one's fellowmen the art of speech, in its infancy, was of infinitely more value to the human race than it is today. Now, we converse mechanically – the more one listens to ordinary conversations the more apparent it becomes that the reasoning faculties of the brain take little part in the direction of the vocal organs. When Tha spoke to Nu and the warriors of his tribe he was constantly required to invent signs and words to carry varying shades of meaning to his listeners. It was great mental exercise for Tha and for his audience as well – men were good listeners in those days; they had to be and they advanced more rapidly in proportion to our advancement, because what little speech they heard meant something – it was too precious to waste, nor could men afford to attend to foolish matters where it required all their eyes as well as their ears and the concentration of the best of their mental faculties to follow the thread of an argument.

Tha stepped to the center of the group of warriors. There was a little open space left there for the speaker. About it squatted the older men. Behind them knelt others, and behind these stood the young men of the tribe of Nu.

Tha uttered a deep rumbling from his chest cavity. He shook his giant frame.

'The ground roars and trembles where we live,' he said. 'The cliffs will fall.' He pointed toward their dwellings, making a gesture with his open palms toward the ground. 'We shall all be killed. Let us go. Let us seek a new place where the ground does not tremble. The beasts are everywhere. Fruit is everywhere. Grain grows in the valley of every river. We may hunt elsewhere as well as here. We shall find plenty to eat. Let us take our women and our children and go out of this place.'

As he spoke he mimicked the hunting of game, the gathering of fruit and grain, the marching and the search for a new home. His motions were both dignified and graceful. His listeners sat in rapt attention. When he had done he squatted down among the older warriors. Then another rose – a very old man. He came to the center of the open space, and told, by word and pantomime, the dangers of migration. He recalled the numerous instances when strangers, in small parties and in great numbers had come too close to the country of Nu, and how they, Nu's warriors, had rushed upon them, slaying all who could not escape.

'Others will do the same to us,' he said, 'if we approach their dwellings.'

When he had sat down Hud pushed through to the center from the ring of younger warriors. Hud desired Nat-ul, the daughter of Tha. Therefore he had two good reasons for espousing the cause of her father. One was that he might ingratiate himself with the older man, and the other was the hope that the tribe might migrate at once while Nu, the son of Nu, was absent, thus giving Hud uninterrupted opportunity to push his suit for the girl.

'Tha has spoken wisely,' he said. 'This land is no longer safe for man or beast. Scarce a moon passes that does not see the ground tremble and crack, and in places have faces of the mountains tumbled away. Any time it may be the turn of our cliff to fall. Let us go to a land where the ground does not tremble. We need not fear the strangers. That is the talk of old men, and women who are big with child. The tribe of Nu is mighty. It can go where it pleases, and slay those who would block its way. Let us do as Tha says, and go away from here at once – another great trembling may come at any moment. Let us leave now, for we have eaten.'

Others spoke, and so great was the fear of the earthquakes among them that there was scarce a dissenting voice – nearly all wished to go. Nu listened with grave dignity. When all had spoken who wished to speak he arose.

'It is best,' he said. 'We will go away—' Hud could scarce repress a smile of elation 'so soon as Nu, my son, returns.' Hud scowled. 'I go to seek him,' concluded Nu.

The council was over. The men dispersed to their various duties. Tha accompanied Nu in search of the latter's son. A party of hunters went north toward the Barren Cliffs, at the foot of which, not far from the sea, one of the tribe had seen a bull mammoth the previous day.

Hud went to his cave and watched his opportunity to see Nat-ul alone. At last his patience was rewarded by sight of her going down toward the spring, which was now deserted. Hud ran after her. He overtook her as she stooped to fill the bladder.

'I want you,' said Hud, coming directly to the point in most primitive fashion, 'to be my mate.'

Nat-ul looked at him for a moment and then laughed full in his face.

'Go fetch the head of Oo and lay it before my father's cave,' she answered, 'and then, maybe, Nat-ul will think about becoming the mate of Hud. But I forgot,' she suddenly cried, 'Hud does not hunt – he prefers to remain at home with the old men and the women and the children while the *men* go forth in search of Gluh.' She emphasized the word men.

The man colored. He was far from being a physical coward – cowards were not bred until a later age. He seized her roughly by the arm.

'Hud will show you that he is no coward,' he cried, 'for he will take you away to be his mate, defying Nu and Tha and Nu, the son of Nu. If they come to take you from him, Hud will slay them all.'

As he spoke he dragged her toward the jungle beyond the spring – the jungle that lay between the cliff and the sea. Nat-ul struggled, fighting to be free; but Hud, a great hand across her mouth and an arm about her body, forged silently ahead with his captive. Beyond the jungle the man turned north along the beach. Now he relaxed his hold upon the girl's mouth.

'Will you come with me?' he asked, 'or must I drag you thus all day?'

'I shall not come willingly,' she replied, 'for otherwise Nu, the son of Nu, nor my father, nor my brother might have the right to kill you for what you have done; but now they may, for you are taking me by force as did the hairy people who lived long time ago take their mates. You are a beast, Hud, and when my men come upon you they will slay you for the beast you are.'

'You will suffer most,' retorted Hud, 'for if you do not come willingly with me the tribe will kill the child.'

'There will be no child,' replied Nat-ul, and beneath her red-doe skin she hugged the stag handle of a stone knife.

Hud kept to the beach to escape detection by the mammoth hunters upon their return from the chase, for they, too, had gone northward; but along the base of the cliffs upon the opposite side of the strip of jungle that extended parallel with the beach to the very foot of the Barren Cliffs, where they jutted boldly out into the Restless Sea half a day's journey northward.

The sun was directly above the two when Hud dragged his unwilling companion up the steep face of the Barren Cliffs which he had determined to cross in search of a secure hiding place, for he knew that he might not return to the tribe for a full moon after the thing that he had done. Even then it might not be safe, for the men of the tribe of Nu had not taken their mates by force for many generations. There was a strong belief among them that the children of women who mated through their own choice were more beautiful, better natured and braver than those whose mothers were little better than prisoners and slaves. Hud hoped, however, to persuade Nat-ul to say that she had run away with him voluntarily, to which there could be no objection. But that might require many days.

From the top of the Barren Cliffs there stretched away toward the north an entirely different landscape than that upon the southern side. Here was a great level plain, dotted with occasional clumps of trees. At a little distance a broad river ran down to the sea, its banks clothed in jungle. Upon the plain, herds of antelope, bison and bos browsed in tall grasses and wild grains. Sheep, too, were there, and rooting just within the jungle were great droves of wild hog. Now and then there would be a sudden stampede among the feeding herbivora as some beast of prey dashed among them. Bleating, bellowing squealing or grunting they would race off madly for a short distance only to resume their feeding and love-making when assured that they were not pursued, though the great carnivore might be standing in full sight of them above the carcass of its kill. But why run further? All about them, in every direction, were other savage, bloodthirsty beasts. It was but a part of their terror stricken lives fleeing hither and thither as they snatched sustenance, and only surviving because they bred more surely than the beasts that preyed upon them and could live further from water.

Hud led Nat-ul down the northern face of the Barren Cliffs, searching for a cavern in which they might make their temporary home. Halfway between the summit and the base he came upon a cave. Before it were strewn gnawed bones of antelope, buffalo and even mammoth. Hud grasped his spear more firmly as he peered into the dark interior. Here was the cave of Ur, the cave-bear. Hud picked up a bone and threw it within. There was no remonstrative growl – Ur was not at home.

Hud pushed Nat-ul within, then he rolled a few large

boulders before the cave's mouth – enough to bar the entrance of the gigantic bear upon his return. After, he crawled through the small opening that he had left. In the dim light of the interior he saw Nat-ul flattened against the further side of the cave. He crossed toward her to take her in his arms.

CHAPTER THREE

THE GREAT CAVE-BEAR

When Nu, the son of Nu, regained consciousness daylight was filtering through several tiny crevices in the debris that blocked the entrance to the cave in which the earthquake had found and imprisoned him. As he sat up, half bewildered, he cast his eyes about the dim interior in search of Nat-ul. Not seeing her he sprang to his feet and searched each corner of the cavern minutely. She was not there! Nu stood for a moment with one hand pressed to his forehead, deep in thought. He was trying to marshal from the recesses of his memory the occurrences of his immediate past.

Finally he recalled that he had set forth from the village of his people in search of Oo, as he had been wont to do often in the past, that he might bring the head of the fierce monster and lay it before the cave of Nat-ul, daughter of Tha. But what had led him to believe that Nat-ul should be there now in the cave beside him? He passed his hand across his eyes, yet the same memory-vision persisted – a confused and chaotic muddle of strange beasts and stranger men, among which he and Nat-ul fled through an unknown world.

Nu shook his head and stamped his foot – it was all a ridiculous dream. The shaking of the earth the previous night, however, had been no dream – this and the fact that he was buried alive were all too self-evident. He remembered that he had not found Oo at home, and when the quake had come he had run into the cave of the great beast to hide from the wrath of the elements.

Now he turned his attention to the broken rock piled before the mouth of the cave. To his immense relief he discovered that it was composed largely of small fragments. These he loosened and removed one by one, and though others continued to roll down from above and take their places for a while, until the cave behind him was half filled with the debris, he eventually succeeded in making an opening of sufficient size to pass his body through into the outer air.

Looking about him he discovered that the quake seemed to have done but little damage other than to the top of the cliff which had overhung before and now had fallen from above, scattering its fragments upon the ledges and at the foot of the escarpment.

For years Oo had laired here. It was here that Nu had sought him since he had determined to win his mate with the greatest of all trophies, but now that his cave was choked with the debris of the cliff top Oo would have to seek elsewhere for a den, and that might carry him far from the haunts of Nu. That would never do at all – Oo must be kept within striking distance until his head had served the purpose for which the troglodyte intended it.

So for several hours Nu labored industriously to remove the rocks from the cave and from the ledge immediately before it, as well as from the rough trail that led up from the foot of the cliff. All the time he kept his spear close to his hand, and his stone ax and knife ready in his gee-string, for at any moment Oo might return. As the great cat had a way of appearing with most uncanny silence and unexpectedness it behooved one to be ever on the alert. But at last the work was completed and Nu set forth to search for a breakfast.

He had determined to await the return of the saber-toothed tiger and have the encounter over for good and all. Had not the young men and women of the tribe begun to smile of late each time that he returned empty handed from the hunt for Oo? None had doubted the sincerity of his desire to meet the formidable beast from which it was no disgrace to fly, for none doubted the courage of Nu; but nevertheless it was humiliating to return always with excuses instead of the head of his quarry.

Nu had scarce settled himself comfortably upon the branch of a tree where he could command the various approaches to the tiger's lair when his keen ear caught the sound of movement in the jungle at his back. The noise was up wind from him and presently the scent of man came down the breeze to the sensitive nostrils of the watcher. Now he was alert in this new direction, every faculty bent to discovering the identity of the newcomers before they sensed his presence.

Soon they came in view – two men, Nu and Tha searching for the former's son. At sight of them, Nu, the son of Nu, called out a greeting.

'Where go Nu and Tha?' he asked, as the two came to a halt beneath his perch.

'They sought Nu, the son of Nu,' replied the young man's father, 'and having found him they return to the dwellings of Nu's people, and Nu, the son of Nu, returns with them.'

The young man shrugged his broad shoulders.

'Nu, the son of Nu, would remain and slay Oo,' he replied.

'Come down and accompany your father,' returned the older man, 'for the people of Nu start today in search of other dwelling where the earth does not shake, or the cliffs crumble and fall.'

Nu slid nimbly to the ground.

'Tell me which way the tribe travels,' said Nu, the son of Nu, 'that I may find them after I have slain Oo, if he returns today. If he does not return today, then will I set out tomorrow after the tribe.'

The young man's father thought in silence for a moment. He was very proud of the prowess of his son. He should be as elated as the young man himself when he returned with the head of the hunter of men and of mammoths. Then, too, he realized the humiliation which his son might feel on being forced to return again without the trophy. He laid his hand upon the young man's shoulder.

'Remain, my son,' he said, 'until the next light. The tribe

will travel north beside the Restless Sea beyond the Barren Cliffs. Because of the old and the babes we shall move slowly. It will be easy for you to overtake us. If you do not come we shall know that Oo was mightier than the son of Nu.'

Without other words the two older men turned and retraced their steps toward the village, while Nu, the son of Nu, climbed again to his perch within the tree.

All day he watched for the return of Oo. The great apes and the lesser apes passed below and above and around him. Sometimes they threw him a word in passing. Below, the woolly rhinoceros browsed and lay down to sleep. A pack of hyenas slunk down from the plateau above the cliffs. They circled the sleeping perissodactyl. The great beast opened its little eyes. Lumberingly it came to its feet, wheeling about until it faced up wind, then, like a mountain run amuck, it charged straight for the line of now growling hyenas. The cowardly brutes leaped aside, and the whole pack closed upon the rear of the rhinoceros. The big beast turned, quick as a cat. Down went his armed snout and one of his tormentors was hurled far aloft, torn by the mighty horn that had pierced him through. Again the rhinoceros wheeled and ran, and again the pack closed in upon him. The jungle swallowed them, but for a long time Nu could hear the savage growls of the pursuing beasts, and the yells of pain as from time to time the rhinoceros turned upon his tormentors.

Then came a cave-bear, lumbering down the face of the cliff. At the mouth of the cave of Oo he halted sniffing about warily, and uttering deep throated growls of rage and hate. Nu listened for the answering challenge of the ancient enemy of Ur, but no sound came. Nu shrugged his shoulders. It was evident that Oo was far away, otherwise he would never have let Ur's challenge go unanswered.

Now the bear had continued his way to the foot of the cliff. He was advancing toward the tree in which Nu sat. At the edge of the jungle the beast halted and commenced to nose in the soft earth for roots. Nu watched him. If not the head of Oo, why not the head of Ur? Oo would not return that day, of that Nu was positive, for it was already late in the afternoon and if the great tiger had been near he would have heard and answered the challenge of the cave-bear.

Nu dropped lightly to the ground upon the opposite side of the tree from Ur. In his right hand he grasped his long, heavy spear. In his left was his stone ax. He approached the huge beast from the rear, coming within a few paces of it before the animal was aware of his presence, for none of the jungle folk moved more noiselessly than primeval man.

But at last Ur looked up, and at the same instant Nu's mighty muscles launched the stone tipped spear. Straight as a bullet it sped toward the breast of the hairy monster, burying itself deep in his body as he lunged forward to seize the rash creature that dared attack him.

Nu held his ground, standing with feet apart and swinging his heavy stone ax to and fro in both hands. The cave-bear rose upon his hind feet as he neared the man, towering high above his enemy's head. With gaping jaws and outstretched paws the terrible beast advanced, now and then tearing at the stout haft of the spear protruding from its breast, and giving tongue to roars of rage and pain that shook the earth.

As the mighty forearms reached for him, Nu dodged beneath them, swinging his ax to the side of the bear's head as he passed. With a howl the beast wheeled and charged in the new direction, but again Nu followed his previous tactics, and again a crushing blow fell upon the side of the cave-bear's jaw.

Blood spurted from the creature's mouth and nostrils, for not only had the stone ax brought blood, but the stone spear had penetrated the savage lungs. And now Ur did what Nu had been waiting for him to do. He dropped upon all fours and raced madly toward his tormentor. The changed position brought the top of the skull within reach of the man's weapon, and this time, as he sidestepped the charge, he brought the ax down full upon the bear's forehead, between his eyes.

Stunned, the beast staggered and stumbled, his nose buried in the trampled mud and grass of the battlefield. Only for an instant would he be thus, and in that instant must

Nu leap in and finish him. Nor did he hesitate. Dropping his ax he sprang upon Ur with his stone knife, and again and again sent the blade into the wild heart. Before the cave-bear regained full consciousness he rolled over upon his side, dead.

For half an hour Nu was busy removing the head, and then he set himself to the task of skinning the beast. His methods were crude, but he worked much faster with his primitive implements than modern man with keen knives. Before another hour had passed he had the skin off and rolled into a bundle, and had cut a great steak from Ur's loin. Now he gathered some dry leaves and tinder and with a sharpened bit of hardwood produced fire by twirling the point vigorously in a tiny hollow scooped from another piece of hard wood. When the blaze had been nursed to a fire of respectable dimensions, Nu impaled the steak upon a small branch and squatting before the blaze grilled his supper. It was half burned and half raw and partially smoked, but that he enjoyed it was evidenced by the fact that he devoured it all.

Afterward he placed the pelt upon his shoulder and set forth upon his return to his people. He returned directly to the cliffs by the Restless Sea, for he did not know whether the tribe had yet left in search of the new camping ground or not. It was night by the time he emerged from the jungle at the foot of the cliff. A cursory exploration showed him that the tribe had gone, and so he crawled into his own cave for the night. In the morning he easily could overtake them.

When Hud crossed the cave toward Nat-ul he had expected to encounter physical resistance, and so he came half crouched and with hands outstretched to seize and subdue her.

'Hud,' said the girl, 'if I come to you willingly will you treat me kindly always?'

The man came to a stop a few feet from his victim. Evidently it was going to be more easy than he had anticipated. He did not relish the idea of taking a she-tiger for mate, and so he was glad to make whatever promises the girl required. Afterward he could keep such as were easiest to keep.

'Hud will be a kind mate,' he answered.

The girl stepped toward him, and Hud met her with encircling arms; but as hers went around him he failed to see the sharp stone knife in Nat-ul's right hand. The first he knew of it was when it was plunged remorselessly into his back beneath his left shoulder blade. Then Hud tried to disengage himself from the girl's embrace, but struggle as he would, she clung to him tenaciously, plunging the weapon time and time again into his back.

He tried to reach her throat with his fingers, but her sharp teeth fastened upon his hand, and then, with his free hand, he beat upon her face, but only for an instant, as the knife found his heart, and with a groan he sank to the rocky floor of the cave.

Without waiting to know that he was dead Nat-ul rushed from the dark interior. Swiftly she scaled the Barren Cliffs and dropped once more into her own valley upon the other side. Along the beach she raced back toward the dwellings of her people, not knowing that at that very moment they were setting out in search of a new home. At mid-afternoon she passed them scarce half a mile away, for they had taken the way that led upon the far side of the jungle that they might meet the returning mammoth hunters, and so Nat-ul came to the deserted caves of her tribe at night-fall only to find that her people had departed.

Supperless, she crawled into one of the smaller and higher caves, for it would be futile to attempt to discover the trail of the departed tribe while night with its darkness and its innumerable horrors enveloped the earth. She had dozed once when she was awakened by the sound of movement upon the face of the cliff. Scarce breathing, she lay listening. Was it man or beast that roamed through the deserted haunts of her tribe? Higher and higher up the face of the cliff came the sound of the midnight prowler. That the creature, whatever it was, was making a systematic search of the caves seemed all too apparent. It would be but a question of minutes before it would reach her hiding place.

Nat-ul grasped her knife more firmly. The sounds ceased upon the ledge directly beneath her. Then, after a few moments they were resumed, but to the girl's relief they now retreated down the steep bluff. Presently they ceased entirely, and though it was hours before she could quiet her fears she at last fell into a deep slumber.

At dawn Nu, the son of Nu, awoke. He rose and stretched himself, standing in the glare of the new sun upon the ledge before his cave. Fifty feet above him slept the girl he loved. Nu gathered up his weapons and his bear skin, and moved silently down to the spring where he quenched his thirst. Then he passed through the jungle to the sea. Here he removed his loin cloth and the skin that covered his shoulders and waded into the surf. In his right hand he held his knife, for great reptiles inhabited the Restless Sea. Carefully he bathed, keeping a wary watch for enemies in the water or upon the land behind. In him was no fear, for he knew no other existence than that which might present at any moment the necessity of battling for his life with some slimy creature of the deep, or equally ferocious denizen of the jungle or the hills. To Nu it was but a part of the day's work. You or I might survive a single day were we suddenly cast back into the primeval savagery of Nu's long dead age, and Nu, if as suddenly transplanted to the corner of Fifth Avenue and Twenty-third Street might escape destruction for a few hours, but sooner or later a trolley car or a taxi would pounce upon him.

His ablutions completed, the troglodyte replaced his loin cloth and his shaggy fur, took up his weapons and his burden and set forth upon the trail of his father's people. And above him, as he passed again along the foot of the cliff, the woman that he loved slept in ignorance of his presence.

When, at last, Nat-ul awoke the sun was high in the heavens. The girl came cautiously down the cliff face, looking first in one direction and then another. Often pausing for several minutes at a time to listen. All about her were the noises of the jungle and the sea and the air, for great birds and horrid winged reptiles threatened primeval men as sorely from above as did the carnivora of the land from his own plane.

She came to the spring in safety, and passed on into the jungle in search of food, for she was half famished. Fruits and vegetables, with grasshoppers, caterpillars and small rodents, and the eggs of birds and reptiles were what she sought, nor was she long in satisfying the cravings of her appetite. Nature was infinitely more bountiful in those days than at the present, for she had infinitely more numerous and often far greater stomachs to satisfy then than now.

Nat-ul passed through the jungle to the beach. She had wanted to bathe, but, alone, she dared not. Now she stood wondering in which direction the tribe had gone. She knew that ordinarily if they had been traveling either north or south they would follow the hard-packed sand of the beach, for there the traveling was easiest, but the tide would have washed away their spoor long before this. She had seen signs of their passage north beside the jungle, but the trail was an old, well worn one traversed daily by many feet, so she had not been able to guess from it that it contained the guide to the direction her people had taken.

As she stood upon the beach trying to reason out her future plans, it became apparent that if the tribe had gone north she would have met them on her return from the Barren Cliffs yesterday, and so, as she had not met them, they must have gone south.

And so she turned her own footsteps south away from her people and from Nu.

CHAPTER FOUR

THE BOAT BUILDERS

Nat-ul kept to the beach as she tramped southward. Upon her right was the jungle, upon her left the great sea, stretching away she knew not whither. To her it represented the boundary of the world – all beyond was an appalling waste of water. To the south-east she could see the outlines of islands. They were familiar objects, yet shrouded in mystery. Often they formed the topic of conversation among her people. What was there upon them? Were they inhabited? And if so, were the creatures men and women like themselves? To Nat-ul they were as full of romantic mystery as are the stars and planets to us, but she knew less of them than we do of the countless brilliant islands that dot the silent sea of space – they were further from Nat-ul and her people than is Mars from us. A boat was as utterly unknown to Nat-ul as was a telescope.

Just beyond a rise of ground ahead of Nat-ul fifty or sixty men, women and children were busy beside a little stream that flowed into the sea. When Nat-ul topped the rise and her eyes fell upon these strangers she dropped suddenly flat upon her belly behind a bush. There she watched the peculiar actions of these people. It was evident that they had but just arrived after a long march. They differed in many ways from any people she had ever seen. Their skins were of the less dangerous animals – those which fed upon grasses. Their head-dresses bore the horn of bulls and antelope, giving them, altogether, a most fearsome aspect.

But it was their habitations and the work upon which they were engaged which caused Nat-ul the greatest wonderment. Their caves were not caves at all. They were constructed of a number of long saplings leaned inward against one another in a circle, and covered with skins and brush, or the great fronds of giant palms as well as those of the plant which is known today as it was in Nat-ul's time as elephant's ear, because of its resemblance to that portion of the great pachyderm.

The weapons of these peoples were unlike those with which Nat-ul was familiar. The stone ax was of a different shape, and the spear was much shorter and stouter, its point being barbed, and having one end of a long, plaited sinew rope tied to it, while the balance of the rope was fastened in a coil at the warrior's side. Nat-ul knew nothing of fisher folk. Her own people often caught fish. Sometimes they speared them with their light spears, but they did not make a business of fishing. So she did not know that the spears of these strangers answered the double purpose of weapons of warfare and harpoon.

What interested her most, however, was the strange work upon which many of the people were engaged. They had cut down a number of large trees, which they had chopped and burned into different lengths, from fifteen to twenty feet. With their stone axes they had hewn away the bark and heavier growth along the upper surfaces of the logs. The softer, pithy centers had been scooped out and fires built within.

Nat-ul could not but wonder at the purpose of all this labor. She saw the men and women tending the fires carefully, extinguishing with water any blaze that seemed threatening to pierce too far from the center of a tree. Deeper and deeper the flames ate until there remained but a thin outer husk of firehardened wood.

So intent was the girl upon the strange sights before, her that she did not note the approach of a tall, young warrior from the jungle at her right and a little behind her. The man was tall and straight. A shaggy bison hide fell from his shoulders, the tail dragging upon the ground behind him. Upon his head the skull of the bull fitted firmly – a primitive helmet – clothed in its dried skin and with the short, stout horns protruding at right angles from his temples.

In his right hand was the stout harpoon and at his waist the coil of sinew rope. The robe, falling away in front, disclosed a well knit, muscular figure, naked but for a loin cloth of doe skin in which was stuck his stone knife and ax.

For several minutes he stood watching the girl, his eyes glowing at the beauties of her profile and lithe, graceful figure. Then, very cautiously, he crept toward her. It was Tur of the Boat Builders. Never in his life had Tur looked upon a more beautiful woman. To see her was to want her. Tur must own her. He was almost upon her when a dried twig snapped beneath his tread.

Like a startled antelope Nat-ul was upon her feet. At the same instant Tur leaped forward to seize her. She was between him and the camp she had been watching. To run toward them would have meant certain capture. Like a shot she wheeled right into Tur's outstretched arms, but as they closed to grasp her they encircled but empty air. Nat-ul had ducked beneath the young warrior's eager embrace and was fleeing north along the beach, like a frightened deer.

After her sprang Tur, calling upon her to stop; but with terror goaded speed the fleet footed Nat-ul raced on. A hundred paces behind her came Tur. For a short distance she might outstrip him, he knew, but in the end his mightier muscles would prevail. Already she was lagging. No longer was the distance between them growing. Soon it would lessen. He would close upon her – and then!

To the north of the Barren Cliffs Nu overtook the tribe of Nu, his father. He came upon them during a period of rest, and as he approached he noted the constraint of their manners as they greeted him. The young women looked at him with sorrowing eyes. His young warrior friends did not smile as he called their names in passing.

Straight to Nu, his father, he went, as became a returning warrior. He found the chief sitting with Tha before a small fire where a ptarmigan, clay wrapped, was roasting.

His father rose and greeted him. There was pleasure in the older man's eyes at sight of his son, but no smile upon his lips. He glanced at the head and pelt of Ur.

'Oo did not return?' he asked.

'Oo did not return,' replied the son.

Nu, the son of Nu, looked about among the women and children and the uneasy warriors. She he sought was not there. His mother came and kissed him as did Una his sister.

'Where is Nat-ul?' asked Nu.

His mother and his sister looked at one another and then at his father. Nu, the chief, looked at Tha. Tha rose and came before the young man. He laid his hand upon the other's shoulder.

'Since your mother bore you,' he said, 'always have I loved you – loved you second only to Aht, my own son. Some day I hoped that you would become my son, for I saw that you loved Nat-ul, my daughter. But now Nat-ul has gone away with Hud. We know not how it happened, but Ra-el, the daughter of Kor, says that she went willingly.'

He got no further.

'It is a lie!' cried Nu, the son of Nu. 'Nat-ul never went willingly with Hud or any other. When did they go? Whither went they? Tell me, and I will follow and bring back Nat-ul, and with her own lips she will give Ra-el the lie. I will bring her back if she still lives, but unless she escaped Hud she is dead, for she would have died rather than mate with another than Nu, the son of Nu. I have spoken. Which way went they?'

No one could tell him. All that they knew was that when the tribe set out from their old dwellings Hud and Nat-ul could not be found, and then Ra-el had come forward and said that the two had fled together. When he questioned Ra-el he could glean nothing more from her, but she stuck obstinately to her assertion that Nat-ul had gone willingly.

'And will Nu, the son of Nu, be such a fool as to follow after a woman who has chosen another mate when there are those as beautiful whom Nu, the son of Nu, could have for the asking?' she said.

At her words the young man saw the motive behind her statement that Nat-ul had run away voluntarily with Hud, and now he was more positive than ever that the girl did not speak the truth. Her words recalled many little occurrences in the past that had slipped by unnoticed at a time when all his thoughts were of the splendid Nat-ul. It was evident that Ra-el would have liked Nu for herself.

The young man returned to his father's side.

'I go,' he said, 'nor shall I return until I know the truth.'

The older man laid his hand upon the shoulder of the younger.

'Go, my son,' he said; 'your father's heart goes with you.'

In silence Nu, the son of Nu, retraced his steps southward toward the Barren Cliffs. It was his intention to return directly to the former dwellings of his people and there search out the spoor of Hud and Nat-ul. A great rage burned in his heart as he thought of the foul deed that Hud had done. The tribe of Nu had progressed far beyond the status of the beasts. They acknowledged certain property rights, among them the inalienable right of the man to his mate, and, going a step further, the right of the woman to mate as she chose. That Nat-ul had chosen to mate with Hud, Nu could not for a moment admit. He knew the courageous nature of the girl, and, knowing it, knew that had she preferred Hud to him she would have mated with the man of her choice openly after the manner of the tribe. No, Nat-ul would never have run off with any man – not even himself.

Halfway up the face of the Barren Cliffs Nu was arrested by a faint moan, coming apparently from a cave at his right. He had no time to devote to the pleasures of the chase, but there was a human note in the sound that he had heard that brought him up all suddenly alert and listening. After a moment it was repeated. No, there could be no doubt of it – that sound came only from a human throat. Cautiously Nu crept toward the mouth of the cave from which the moaning seemed to issue. At the entrance he came to a sudden halt, at the sight that met his eyes.

There, in the half light of the entrance, lay Hud in a pool of blood. The man was breathing feebly. Nu called him by name. Hud opened his eyes. When he saw who stood over him he shrugged his shoulders and lay still, as though to say, the worst has already been done to me – you can do no more.

'Where is Nat-ul?' asked Nu.

Hud shook his head. Nu knelt beside him raising his head in his arms.

'Where is Nat-ul, man?' he cried, shaking the dying warrior. 'Tell me before you die. I do not ask if she went with you willingly, for I know that she did not – all I ask is what have you done with her? Does she live? And if she lives, where is she?'

Hud tried to speak. The effort cost him dear. But at last he managed to whisper a few words.

'She – did – this,' he panted. 'Then she – went – away. I don't – know—' he gasped, and died.

Nu dropped him back upon the stone floor of the cave and ran out upon the ledge. He searched about the face of the cliff, even going down upon all fours and creeping from ledge to ledge, oftentimes with his nose close to the trail – sniffing.

After half an hour of going back and forth over the same ground and following a rocky ascent upward toward the summit of the cliff a dozen times, as though proving and reproving the correctness of his deductions, Nu at last set forth across the Barren Cliffs and down onto the beach beside the Restless Sea.

Here he found the spoor more plainly marked in many places above high tide where Nat-ul's little sandals had left their legible record in the soft loam or upon the higher sand that the water had not reached. The way led southward, and southward hurried Nu, the son of Nu. Straight to the old dwellings led the trail. There Nu found evidence that Nat-ul had spent the night in a cave above the one in which he had slept. There was the bed of grasses and a trace of the delicate aroma that our blunted sense of smell could never have detected, but which was plain to Nu, and deliciously familiar.

A pang of regret seized him as he realized that his Nat-ul had been so close to him, and that he had unwittingly permitted her to remain alone and unprotected amidst the countless dangers of their savage world, and to go forth, none knew where, into other myriad dangers.

Returning to the foot of the cliff he once more came upon the girl's spoor. Again it led south along the beach. Swiftly he followed it until it stopped behind a little clump of bushes at the top of a rise in the ground. Before Nu realized that this was the southern limit of the trail he had seen the village beyond and the people engaged in what to him seemed a strange occupation. He knew that the same sight had brought Nat-ul to a halt a few hours before, and now he saw where she had lain upon her belly watching, just as he was watching. For a few minutes he lay watching the workers and seeking through the little cluster of skin and thatch shelters for some sign that Nat-ul was a prisoner there.

Nu had never seen a boat or guessed that such a thing might be. His people had been hunters from time immemorial. They had come down from the great plateaux far inland but a few generations since. Then, for the first time, had his forefathers seen the ocean. As yet they had not met with any need that required them to navigate its waters, nor had they come in contact with the Boat Builders who dwelt far south at the mouth of a great river that emptied into the Restless Sea.

Now, for the first time, Nu saw both the boats and the Boat Builders. For the first time he saw artificial shelters, and to Nu they seemed frail and uncomfortable things by comparison with his eternal caves. The Boat Builders had been several days in this new camp. What had driven them so far north of their ancestral home, who may guess? A tribal feud, perhaps; or the birth of a new force that was to drive them and their progeny across the face of the world in restless wanderings to the end of time – the primitive wanderlust from which so many of us suffer, and yet would not forego.

Nu saw that of all the workers one tall young giant labored most rapidly. His haste seemed almost verging upon frenzy. Nu wondered what he could be about upon the felled tree trunk that required so much exertion. Nu did not like work of that nature. It is true that he had never done any manual labor outside the needs of the chase, but intuitively he knew that he disliked it. He was a hunter, a warrior, and even then, in his primitive and untutored mind, there arose a species of contempt for the drudge. At last, tiring of watching, he turned his attention again to the spoor he had been following. Where had Nat-ul gone after lying here behind these bushes?

Nu crawled about until he saw evidences of the girl's quick leap to her feet and her rapid flight. Then it was he came upon the footprints of Tur. Now Nu's blood ran hot. It surged through his heart and pounded against his temples – Nat-ul, his Nat-ul, was in danger!

He saw where the girl had dodged past the man. He saw, distinctly in the sand, the marks of Tur's quickly turning footsteps as he wheeled in pursuit. He saw that the two had been running rapidly along the beach toward the north – the man following the girl, and then, to his surprise, he saw that the man had come to a sudden stop, had taken a few steps forward, stood for some time looking seaward and then turned and raced back toward the strange camp at breakneck speed.

And the girl's trail had continued toward the north for perhaps a hundred paces beyond the point at which the man had halted. Nu followed it easily – they were fresh signs since the last high tide, alone and uncrossed upon a wide stretch of smooth, white sand.

Nu followed the dainty imprints of Nat-ul's swiftly flying little feet for a hundred paces beyond the end of the man's pursuit – and came to a dead, bewildered halt. The footprints ended abruptly upon the beach midway between the ocean and the jungle. About them was only an expanse of unbroken sand. They simply ceased, that was all. They did not double back upon themselves. They did not enter the ocean. They did not approach the jungle. They stopped as though Nat-ul had suddenly been swallowed by a great hole in the beach. But there was no hole. Nu halted and looked about in every direction. There was no trace of any living thing about. Where had Nat-ul gone? What had become of her? Had the footprints of the man who pursued her reached the point upon the sand where hers ended, Nu would have concluded that he had picked her up and carried her back to his village; but the man had been a hundred paces behind Nat-ul when her trail ceased, nor had he approached closer to the spot at any time. And when he had returned to his village he had done so at a rapid run, and the lightness of his spoor indicated that he had not been burdened with a heavy load.

For some time Nu stood in bewildered thought, but at last he turned back toward the village of the Boat Builders. Nu knew little of the super-natural, and so he turned first to the nearest material and natural cause of Nat-ul's disappearance that he could conceive – the man who had pursued her. And that man had returned to the village of the strangers who were diligently burning and scooping the hearts out of felled trees.

Nu returned to the vantage of the bush before the village. Here he lay down again to watch – he was positive that in some way these people were responsible for the disappearance of Nat-ul. They knew where she was, and, judging by his own estimate of the girl, he knew that the man who had seen her and pursued her would not lightly relinquish his attempts to obtain her. Nu had seen the women of the strangers – beside his Nat-ul they looked like the shes of the ape-folk. No, the man would seek to follow and capture the radiant stranger. Nu wished that he could guess which of the men it was who had chased Nat-ul. Something told him that it was the young giant who worked with such feverish haste, so Nu watched him most closely.

At last Tur's boat was completed. The centers of the trees the Boat Builders selected for their craft is soft, and easily burned and scooped. The fires kindled in the hollowed trunk served a double purpose – they ate away the harder portions nearer the outside and at the same time tended to harden what remained. The result was a fairly light and staunch dug-out.

When Tur's boat was finished he called to several of the other workers. These came, and, lending a hand with Tur, dragged the hollowed log down to the water. One of the women came with a long stick, larger at one end than the other, and with the large end flattened upon both sides. It was a paddle. Tur tossed this into the boat and then running through the surf he launched his primitive craft upon the crest of a receding roller, leaped in, and seizing the paddle struck out vigorously against the next incoming wave.

Nu watched him with wide eyes. His estimate of the man rose in leaps and bounds. Here was sport! And Nu did not have to attempt the feat he had witnessed to know that it required skill and courage. Only a brave man would venture the perils of the awful waters. Where was he going? Nu saw that he paddled straight out into the sea. In the distance were the islands. Could he be going to these? Nu, from childhood, had always longed to explore those distant lands of mystery. These people had found a way. Nu had learned something – an aeroplane could not have presented greater wonders to him than did this crude dug-out.

For a while he watched the man in the little boat. They grew smaller and smaller as wind, tide and the sturdy strokes of the paddler carried the hollowed log farther out to sea. Then Nu turned his attention once more to the other workers. He saw that they, too, were rapidly completing their boats. They were talking back and forth among themselves, raising their voices, as they were scattered over a considerable distance about the village. Nu caught a word now and then. The language was similar to his own. He discovered that they were talking about the man who had just departed, and about his venture. Nu wanted to hear more. He crept cautiously through the dense vegetation to the little clearing the strangers had made about their shelters. As he peered through the curtain of tangled creepers that hid him from their view, he saw the camp more closely. He saw the ring of ashes that surrounded it – the remains of the nocturnal fires that kept off the beasts of prey by night. He saw the cooking fire before each rude shelter. He saw pots of clay – something new to him. He saw the women and the children and the men. They did not differ greatly from his own people, though their garments and weapons were dissimilar. And now he could hear all their conversation.

'She must be beautiful,' a man was saying, 'or Tur would not venture across this strange water to those unknown lands in search of her,' and he grinned broadly, casting a knowing glance at a young woman who suckled a babe, as she sat scraping, scraping, scraping with a bit of sharpened flint upon the hide of an aurochs, pegged out upon the ground before her.

The young woman looked up with an ugly scowl.

'Let him bring her back,' she cried, 'and she will no longer be beautiful. This will I do to her face,' and she fell to scraping viciously upon the skin.

'Tur was very angry when she escaped him,' continued the man. 'He almost had his hands upon her; but he will find her, though whether there will be enough left of her to bring back is hard to say – I, myself, rather doubt it and think that it is a foolish thing for Tur to waste his time thus.'

Nu was nonplussed. Could it be possible that the man they called Tur was pursuing Nat-ul to those distant islands? How could Nat-ul be there? It was impossible. And yet there seemed little doubt from the conversation he had overheard that the man was following *some* woman across the water to the mysterious lands – a woman he had just surprised and chased that very day, and who had eluded him. Who else could it be but Nat-ul?

CHAPTER FIVE

NU'S FIRST VOYAGE

Presently all the boats were completed, and the men dragged them one by one down close to the water. In them they placed their paddles, their axes and their harpoons, just as Tur had before he departed. Nu watched them with feverish interest. At last all have been launched, and are being paddled vigorously beyond the surf. In the comparatively smoother water the boats turn toward the north and south, scattering. Evidently they are not bound for the distant islands. Nu sees a warrior rise suddenly in the bow of one of the boats and hurl his spear quickly into the water. Immediately there is a great commotion in the boat and in the water beside it. There are three men in each boat. Two in the boat Nu is watching, paddle frantically away from the thing that lashes the sea beside them. Nu guessed what had occurred. The spearman had buried his weapon in some huge creature of the deep, and the battle was on. They were too far out for Nu to see the details of the conflict, but he saw the boat towed swiftly by the wounded creature as it raced toward the open sea. He saw the boat pulled closer alongside and another spear hurled into the fleeing thing. He understood now why these men tied their spear-heads to long ropes. He saw the sudden commotion in the dug-out as the hunted turned upon the hunters. He saw the swift stroke of a mighty flipper as it rose from the water and fell with awful fury across the boat. He saw the other boats hurrying toward the scene of battle; but before they reached the spot all was quiet save for two pieces of bobbing tree trunk and the head and shoulders of a single man who clung to one of them. A few minutes later he was dragged into another boat and the fleet dispersed again to search out other prey.

Soon all were out of sight beyond a promontory except a single craft which fished before the village. These men evidently sought less formidable game, and Nu could see that from the teeming sea they were dragging in great fish almost as rapidly as they could hurl their weapons. Soon the boat was completely filled, and with their great load the men paddled slowly inshore.

As they came a sudden resolution formed in Nu's mind. The sight of the dangerous sport upon the waters had filled him with a strong desire to emulate these strangers, but greater than that was the power of another suggestion which the idea held forth.

As the men dragged the boat upon the beach the women came down to meet them, carrying great bags of bull hide sewn with bullock sinew. Into these they gathered the fish and dragged their loads over the ground toward their camp.

The men, their day's work evidently finished, stretched out beneath the shade of trees to sleep. This was the time! Nu moved stealthily to his hands and knees. He grasped his long spear and his stone ax tightly in his hands. The boat lay upon the open beach. There was no near point where he might reach it undetected by the women. The alternative rather appealed to Nu's warlike nature. It was nothing less than rushing directly through the village.

He came to his feet and advanced lightly among the shelters. No need to give the alarm before he was detected. He was directly behind the young woman who scraped the aurochs' skin. She did not hear his light footfall. The baby, now sitting by her side playing with the aurochs' tail, looked up to see the stranger close upon him. He lunged toward his mother with a lusty shriek. Instantly the camp was in commotion. No need now for stealth. With a war whoop that might have sprung from a score of lusty lungs Nu leaped through the village among the frightened women and the startled men, awakened rudely from their sleep.

Straight toward the boat ran Nu, and upon his heels raced the three warriors. One was coming toward him from the side. He was quite close, so close that he came upon Nu at the same instant that the latter reached the boat. The two fell upon one another with their great axes, but Nu, the son of Nu, was a mighty warrior. He dodged the blow of the other's ax, and before his adversary could recover himself to deliver a second Nu's weapon fell upon his skull, crushing it as if it had been an egg shell.

Now Nu seized the boat and dragged it toward the water as he had seen the strangers do. But he had taken but a half dozen steps when he was forced to turn and defend himself against the remaining warriors. With savage howls they were upon him, their women huddled upon the beach behind them shouting wild cries of encouragement to their men and defiance to the enemy. Nu abandoned the boat and rushed to meet his antagonists. His long spear, thrown with the power of the foremost Boat Builder, who was upon the point of hurling his stout harpoon at Nu. Down went the harpooner. Up rose a chorus of howls and lamentations from the women. Now the third warrior closed upon the troglodyte. It was too close for spear work, and so the fellow dropped his heavy weapon and leaped to close quarters with his knife. Down the two men went into the knee deep water, striking at one another with their knives as they sought death holds with their free hands. A great roller rumbled in upon them, turning them over and over as it carried them up the beach. Still they fought, sputtering and choking in the salty brine, but when the wave receded it left a corpse behind it upon the beach, stabbed through and through the great hairy chest by the long, keen knife of Nu, the son of Nu.

The cave man rose, dripping, to his feet and turned back toward the sea. The roller had carried the boat out with it. The women, furious now at the death of their three men, rushed forward to drag down the victor. Savage creatures they were, but little less sinister than their males. Their long hair streamed in the wind. Their faces were distorted by rage and hatred. They screamed aloud their taunts and insults and challenges; but Nu did not wait to battle with them. Instead he dove into the surf and struck out for the drifting boat. His spear was lost, but he clung to his ax. His knife he had returned to his gee-string.

They ran into the water to their waists, but Nu was beyond their reach. In a moment more he had come to the side of the boat. Tossing in his ax he clambered over the side, scarce escaping overturning the hollowed log. Once safely within he took up the paddle, an unaccustomed implement, and, fashioning his strokes after those of the men he had watched, he made headway from the shore.

The tide and the wind helped him, but he found, too, that he quickly mastered the art of paddling. First he discovered that when he paddled exclusively upon the side of his spear hand the boat turned in the opposite direction, and so he understood why the boatmen had paddled alternately upon one side and the other. When he did this the craft kept a straighter course in the direction he wished to go – the distant land of mystery.

Halfway across the water that spread between the mainland and the nearest island a monstrous shape loomed suddenly close to the boat's side. A long neck surmounted by a huge reptilian head shot above the surface, and wide gaping jaws opened to seize the paddler. Protruding eyes glared down upon him, and then the thing struck. Nu dodged to one side and struck back with his knife. With a hiss and scream the creature dove beneath the surface only to reappear a moment later upon the opposite side of the boat. Blood flowed from the knife wound in its neck. Again it snapped at the man, again the knife found its neck as Nu crouched to one side to elude the gaping jaws. Once more the thing dove, and almost simultaneously a mighty tail rose high out of the water above the man's head. Nu seized the paddle and drove the boat forward just as that terrific engine of destruction fell with a mighty whack upon the very spot the boat had quit. The blow, had it touched the craft, would have splintered it into firewood. For a few minutes the sea was churned to white, crimson stained by the creature's blood, as it thrashed about in impotent fury. Then, as Nu paddled away, the raging ceased and the great carcass floated upon its side.

On went Nu, paddling with redoubled energy toward the

distant goal. What he expected to find at his journey's end he could not believe, yet what else was drawing him through countless dangers across the face of the terrible waters? The man, Tur, had come hither. He it was who had pursued Nat-ul. Was he still pursuing her? That he was following some woman Nu was positive from the fragments of conversation he had overheard, and yet though try as he would to believe it he could not make his judgment accept as a possibility the chance that it was really Nat-ul whom the man expected to find upon this distant land.

The wind had risen considerably since Nu set out upon his perilous journey. Already the waves were running high, tipped with white. That the island lay straight before the wind was all that saved the rude craft from instant annihilation. All about him the sea was alive with preying monsters. Titanic duels were in progress upon every hand, as the ferocious reptilia battled over their kills, or, turning from the chase, fell upon one another in frenzied joy of battle while their fortunate quarry swam rapidly away.

Through innumerable dangers swept the little tree-trunk skiff to be deposited at last upon the surf beaten beach of the nearest island. Scarce had Nu landed and dragged his boat above the rollers when he descried another boat a short distance from his own. That this belonged to the man, Tur, he had no doubt, and seizing his ax he hastened to it to pick up and follow the other's spoor wherever it might lead.

Clean cut and distinct in the sand Nu found the impress of Tur's sandals, nor did it require a second glance at them to convince the troglodyte that they had been made by the same feet that had pursued Nat-ul upon the mainland beach.

The trail led around a rocky promontory into a deep and somber gorge. Up the center of this it followed the course of a rapid brook, leaping downward toward the sea. From time to time the man had evidently essayed to scale the cliffs, first upon one side and then upon the other, but each time he had abandoned the attempt before the difficulties and dangers of the precipitous crags.

To Nu the ascent would have proved a simple matter, and so he wondered why the man had turned back each time after clambering but a short distance from the base of the cliffs; but Tur was not a cliff dweller. His peoples had come from a great, level river valley beside the sea – from a country where cliffs and natural caves were the exception rather than the rule, so he had had but little practice in climbing of that sort.

Finally, at the head of the ravine, he had been forced to climb or retrace his steps, and here, at last, he had managed to clamber out upon the table land that stretched beyond the summit. Across this the trail led, turning suddenly toward the west at the edge of another ravine. The abruptness with which the spoor wheeled to the right indicated to Nu that something had suddenly attracted the man's attention toward the new direction and that he had proceeded at a rapid run to investigate. Could he here have discovered the woman he sought? Was he already in pursuit of Nat-ul? – if it was, indeed, she. Was he even now in possession of her?

Nu, too, wheeled to the west and raced rapidly along the well-marked trail. Since he had come upon the signs of Tur, Nu's speed had been infinitely greater than that of the Boat Builder. This his woodcraft told him, so he knew that he was constantly gaining upon the man who was still unconscious of the fact that he was being pursued.

Down the steep side of the ravine Tur must have slid and rolled in a most reckless fashion. At the bottom was a dense forest through which the trail led back toward the sea, after the man had made a series of frantic but futile attempts to scale the opposite heights.

What had he seen or heard or followed that had led him to make such desperate attempts to gain the opposite summit? Should Nu follow him down the ravine, or clamber to the vantage point the other had been unable to reach?

For an instant the troglodyte hesitated. Then he wheeled toward the cliff, and with the agility of long practice backed by ages of cliff dwelling forebears he clambered rapidly upward. At times he was forced to leap for a projecting rock above his head, dangling out over space as he drew himself, by mighty biceps and forearm, to the tiny foothold it afforded. Again, a gnarled root or a small crevice aided him in his ascent, until presently he crawled over the brow and stood erect once more on level ground.

Nu looked about, warily – there was no sign of the man or the woman. Then he examined the ground in ever enlarging circles, but no spoor such as he sought rewarded his eager eyes.

He had about decided to return to the bottom of the ravine and follow Tur's spoor when, clear and shrill from the west, there came to his ears the scream of a woman in distress.

And scarce had its first note risen upon the air than Nu, the son of Nu, was dashing madly in the direction of the sound.

CHAPTER SIX

THE ANTHROPOID APES

As Nat-ul, surprised by Tur in her spying upon the village of the Boat Builders, fled north along the beach she had little hope of permanently distancing her pursuer. But she could do no less than flee, hoping against hope, that some chance accident might save her from capture.

It was in her mind to dodge into the jungle where it came down close to the water a quarter of a mile ahead of her. Here she might elude the man and reach the cliffs that lay a short distance inland. Once there, there was an excellent chance of hiding from him or holding him off with pieces of rock until nightfall. Then she would retrace her steps northward, for it was evident that her people had not traveled in this direction.

The jungle was already quite close, but, on the other hand, the man was gaining upon her. Could she reach the tangled screen in time to elude him before he should be upon her? At least she could do no less than try.

Suddenly from directly above her head came a loud

flapping of great wings. A black shadow fell upon the sand about her. She glanced upward, and the sight that met her eyes froze her brave heart in terror. There, poised just above her ready to strike with its mighty talons, hovered one of those huge flying reptiles, that even in Nat-ul's day were practically extinct – a gigantic pterodactyl.

The man behind her screamed a shout of warning. He launched his barbed spear for the great creature, catching it in the fatty portion of the long tail, near the body. With a whistling scream of pain and rage the hideous thing swooped down upon the girl beneath. Nat-ul felt the huge talons close upon her body. The heavy hide that covered her kept them from piercing through to her flesh as the pterodactyl rose swiftly, bearing her victim with her.

For a moment Nat-ul had battled and struggled for freedom, but almost at once she had realized the futility of her pitiful efforts. In that awful clutch even the cave-bear or the bull bos would have been helpless. Now she hung inert and limp, waiting for the end. She could not even draw her stone knife, for one of the great talons was closed tightly over it where it rested in the cord that supported her loin cloth.

Below her she could see the tossing waters. The thing was bearing her far out from shore. The great wings flapped noisily above her. The long neck and the hideous head were stretched far forward as the creature flew in a straight line, high in air.

Presently the girl saw land ahead. Terror filled her heart as she realized that the thing was bearing her to the mysterious country that lay far out upon the bosom of the Restless Sea. She had dreamed of this strange, unattainable country. There were stories among her people of the awful creatures that dwelt within it. She had sometimes longed to visit it, but always with the brave warriors of her tribe to protect her. To come thus alone to the terrifying shore, in the clutches of the most fearsome beast that terrified primeval man was beyond conception. Her mind was partially stupefied by the enormity of the fate that had overwhelmed her.

Now the great reptile was above the nearest island. A

jagged, rocky hill raised its bare summit in a huge index finger that pointed straight into the air far above the surrounding hill tops and the dense vegetation of the encircling jungle. Toward this the creature bore its prey. As it hovered above the rocky pinnacle Nat-ul glanced fearfully downward. Directly below her her horrified sight fell upon the goal toward which her captor had been winging its rapid way – upon the cruel and hideous fate that awaited her there.

Craning their long necks upward from a cup-like nest of mud matted grasses three young pterodactyls shrilled and hissed in anticipatory joy at their returning mother and the food she brought them.

Several times the adult circled above the young, dropping lower and lower toward the nest in a diminishing spiral. For a second she hovered almost at rest, a few feet above them. Then she loosed her hold upon Nat-ul, dropping her squarely amongst her wide-jawed progeny, and with a final wheel above them soared away in search of her own dinner.

As Nat-ul touched the nest three sets of sharp toothed jaws snapped at her simultaneously. The creatures were quite young, but for all of that they were formidable antagonists, with their many teeth, their sharp talons and their strong tails.

The girl dodged the first assault and drew her knife. Here was no time or place for hysteria or nerves. Death, unthinkably horrible, was upon her. Her chances of escape were practically non-existent, and yet, so strong is the instinct of self-preservation, Nat-ul battled as heroically as though safety depended upon a single lucky knife thrust.

And, though she knew it not, so it did. The three heads were close together as the three monsters sought greedily to devour the tender morsel brought to them by their parent. Nat-ul for a moment eluded the snapping jaws of the awkward young, and then as the three heads came together in a mad attempt to seize her she plunged her blade into two of the long, scraggy necks. Instantly the wounded creatures set up a chorus of whistling shrieks. Their minute brains told them only that they had been hurt, and with bestial fury they set upon one another, each attributing its pain to one of its fellows. Instantly the nest became a mad whirling of wings, tails and hideous jaws. The two that had been wounded set upon each other, and the third, ignoring Nat-ul, fell upon the two contestants with impartial fury.

Taking advantage of their distraction the girl clambered quickly over the side of the nest. Below her the sheer side of the lofty pinnacle dropped fearfully downward a hundred feet. Vertical crevices and slight protuberances of harder rocks that had withstood the ravages of time and the elements afforded the only means of descent. But death, certain and terrible, lay in the nest. Below, there was some hope, however slight.

Clinging to the outside of the nest Nat-ul lowered her body until her feet found a precarious foothold upon a slightly jutting surface of the spire-like needle. Slowly she lowered herself, clinging desperately to each crevice and outcropping. Time and time again it seemed that she must give up, and cling where she was until, exhausted, she toppled to the depth below. Twice she circled the rocky finger in search of a new foothold further down, and each time, when hope seemed hopeless, she had found some meager thing, once only a little rounded roughness, to which her hand or foot could cling a few inches further away from the awful nest above her.

And so at last she came to the base of the gigantic needle, but even here she could not rest. At any moment the mighty mother might return and snatch her back once more to the horrors of her slimy nest.

The descent of the lower summit was, in places, but little less hazardous than that of the surmounting spire; but finally it was accomplished and Nat-ul found herself in a broad ravine, densely wooded. Here she lay down upon the grass to rest, for her labors had exhausted her. She knew not what other dangers menaced her; but for the moment she was numb to further terror. Pillowing her head upon her arm she fell asleep.

About her were the million sounds of the jungle – the lesser animals, the birds, the insects, the swaying branches.

They but lulled her to deeper slumber. The winds blowing up the ravine from the sea, fanned her cheek. It moved the soft, luxuriant hair that fell about her shoulders. It soothed and comforted her, but it did not whisper to her of the close-set wicked eyes that peered out of the trees upon her. It did not warn her of the drooling jaws, the pendulous lower lip, the hairy breast beneath which a savage heart beat faster as the little eyes feasted upon her form. It did not tell her that a huge body had slipped from a nearby tree and was slinking toward her. It did not tell her; but a broken twig, snapping beneath the wary foot of the stalker, did.

Among the primordial there was no easy transition from sleep to wakefulness. There could not be for those who would survive. As the twig snapped Nat-ul was upon her feet facing the new danger that menaced her. She saw a great man-like form slinking toward her. She saw the reddish hair that covered the giant body. She saw the pig eyes and the wolf fangs, the hulking slouch of the heavy torso upon the short, crooked legs. And seeing, all in one swift glance, she turned and fled up the face of the cliff down which she had so recently descended.

As she clambered swiftly aloft the creature behind her rushed forward in pursuit, and behind him came a half dozen others like him. Nat-ul knew them as the hairy, tree people. They differed from the greater ape-folk in that they went always upon two legs when on the ground, and when they were killed and cut up for food they yielded one less rib than their apish prototype. She knew how terrible it was to fall into their hands – worse than the fate that had almost claimed her in the lofty nest, far above.

A hundred feet up the cliff side Nat-ul paused to look back. A dozen yards below her was the hairy one. The girl loosened a bit of rock and hurled it down upon him. He dodged it, and with a shrill scream continued the pursuit. Upward she fled for another hundred feet. Again she paused to look downward. The tree-man was gaining on her. She loosened a bit of quartz and dropped it upon him. Just below him were six others. The missile struck her foremost pursuer. He toppled for an instant, and then tumbled backward upon those behind him. He knocked one from a scant handhold upon the precipitous cliff, and the two dashed violently downward toward the jagged rocks at the bottom.

With an exultant taunt upon her lips Nat-ul resumed her upward flight. Now she came to a point near the summit. The hillside was less steep. Here she could go with only occasional use of her hands. Halfway up, her foot slipped upon a loose, round rock. She fell heavily to the ground, clutching for support as she did so. The few rocks that met her hands gave way beneath her weight. With sickening velocity she hurtled down toward the brink of the perpendicular cliff face – toward mangled, tortured death beside the bodies of the two who had preceded her to the same destruction.

Above the brink of the chasm the first of the remaining pursuers was emerging. He was directly in the path of Nat-ul's swiftly rolling body. It struck him in his hairy breast, hurling him backward into the precipice, to his death. But his body had served a purpose. It had broken the velocity of the girl's fall, so that now she but rolled gently over the edge of the cliff, clutching at the top as she went, and thus further diminishing her speed.

Directly below the summit lay a narrow ledge. Upon this Nat-ul came almost to a full stop, but there was nothing there upon which she could gain a handhold, and so she toppled slowly over the edge – into the arms of another of the man-apes.

Close beside him was one of his fellows, and a little way below the third who remained of the original six. The nearer clutched at Nat-ul to drag her from the arms of her captor, who drew back with bared fangs and menacing growl. But the other was insistent. Evidently he desired the prey fully as much as he who had obtained it. He came closer. The ledge upon which they stood was very narrow. A battle there would have meant death for all three.

With a cat-like leap the creature that held Nat-ul in his arms sprang to one side, turned, and with the strength and agility of a chamois leaped down the steep cliff-face. In his path was the remaining tree-man. To have met that charge would have meant being catapulted to the bottom of the ravine. Wisely, the man-ape sidestepped, but immediately the two had passed he fell into pursuit of them. Behind him came the other that Nat-ul's captor had eluded.

There ensued a mad chase that often blanched the cheek of the almost fearless cave girl. From the base of the cliffs the man-ape leaped across the intervening jungle toward the trees. To the lower branches of these he took without lessening his speed in the least. He almost flew, so swiftly he passed through the tangled mazes of the primeval forest.

Close behind him, screaming and roaring came his two fellows, intent upon robbing him of his prey. He carried Nat-ul across one shoulder, gripping her firmly with a gigantic hand. She could plainly see the pursuers behind them. They were gaining on their burdened fellow. Already the foremost was reaching out to clutch the girl. Her captor shooting a quick glance rearward discovered the imminence of his despoilment. Wheeling suddenly upon the precarious trail he snapped viciously at the nearer pursuer, who, with bared fangs and growling horribly, retreated out of reach. Then the creature recommenced his flight only to be at once pursued again by his two kinsmen.

Up and down the jungle the savage trio raced. Twice they crossed the heights separating one ravine from another. More and more insistent became the pursuers. Oftener the captor was forced to halt with his prize and fight off first one of them and then the other. At last, at the edge of the jungle close to the mouth of a narrow, rocky gorge the beast went mad with rage. He wheeled suddenly upon his pursuers, hurled Nat-ul heavily to the ground, and charged, roaring and foaming, upon them.

They were running side by side, and so quick was the offensive movement of their fellow that they had no time to dodge him. His great hands seized them and then all three went to the earth, tearing at one another, burying their formidable tusks in throat and breast, and all the while keeping up a terrific growling and roaring.

Warily Nat-ul raised herself upon all fours. Her eyes were fastened intently upon the three savage beasts. They paid no attention to her. It was evident that their every faculty was wholly engaged in the life and death struggle upon which they had entered. Nat-ul came to her feet and without another backward glance fled into the narrow gorge behind her. She ran as swiftly as she could that she might put as great a distance as possible between herself and the horrid beasts that battled for her. Where the gorge led she had no conception. What other horrors lay at its end she could not guess. She only knew that hope had almost left her, for that she ever could regain the mainland she had not the faintest belief. Nor could her people succor her even should they discover her whereabouts, which in itself was equally beyond the pale of probability. That she could long survive the dangers of the mysterious country she doubted. Even a mighty warrior, fully armed, would fare ill in this place of terror. What, indeed, was to become of a girl armed only with a knife!

That Nu already was searching for her she did not doubt; but long ere this the tide had washed the imprint of her sandals from the sandy beach. Where would he search? And even had he followed her spoor before the tide had erased it how could he guess what had befallen her, or interpret the sudden ending of her trail in the center of the beach?

The stranger had seen the winged reptile pounce upon her and bear her away; but even if Nu should come upon him how could he learn of the truth, since the moment that the two met they would fall upon one another in mortal combat, as was the way of strangers then.

Or if, by any chance, Nu discovered that she had been carried to the mysterious country how could he follow, even though he believed, against all reason, that she still lived?

No, there seemed no hope anywhere upon Nat-ul's horizon, or below it. There was nothing left for her but to battle for survival, pitting her wits and her agility against the brute force and cunning of the brutes that would menace her to the end of her days – the end that could not be far distant.

The windings of the gorge as she traversed it downward had shut off the louder sounds of the combat raging behind her, though still she could hear an occasional roar, or shriller scream of pain. She hoped that they would fight until all were dead. Otherwise the survivor would continue the pursuit.

As she stopped once to listen that she might know the three were still engaged in battle she turned her eyes backward up the gorge, so that, for the moment, she failed to see that she had reached the end of the narrow canyon and that the beach and the sea lay before her. Nor did she see the figure of the man who came to a sudden stop at the gorge's mouth as his eyes fell upon her, nor the quick movement that took him behind a projecting boulder.

Satisfied that she was not as yet being pursued Nat-ul resumed her way down the rocky trail. As she turned she saw the sea, and, far away, the mainland across the water. She hurried onward toward the beach, that she might reach a point as close as possible to her beloved country.

As she passed the boulder behind which the man hid the scraping of a pebble beneath his sandal attracted her attention. She wheeled toward him and then turned to fly; but he was too close. Already he had leaped for her. One brawny hand closed in her flowing hair, the other grasped the wrist of the upraised hand in which the long knife of the girl had flashed above him with incredible swiftness.

He laughed in her face – it was the stranger who had pursued her upon the mainland beach – and then he drew her toward him. Nat-ul fought like a tigress, and once she screamed.

CHAPTER SEVEN

THE BEAST-FIRES

Tur carried the girl, still struggling and fighting, toward his boat. For the first time he saw the boat that had brought Nu, and wondered at the presence of another craft. Who could it be? A closer inspection revealed that the boat was one that had just been fashioned by others of his own tribe. Some of the men must have followed him. Still clasping Nat-ul firmly as he stood ankle deep in the water beside his boat he raised his voice in a loud halloo.

Presently a clattering of falling stones from the cliff facing the beach attracted the attention of Tur and the girl. Already halfway down, the figure of an agile giant was leaping toward them in descent. From his shoulders fluttered the skin of a cave-lion. From his shock of black hair a single long feather rose straight and defiantly aloft.

A single glance revealed to Tur the fact that this was no member of his tribe. It was a stranger, and so an enemy. Nat-ul recognized Nu at once. She gave a little cry of delight at sight of him, a cry that was answered by a shout of encouragement from Nu. Tur threw the girl roughly into the bottom of the boat, holding her there with one hand, though she fought bitterly to escape, while with his free hand he dragged first his boat and then Nu's out into deeper water.

Handicapped though he was, Tur worked rapidly, for he was at home in the surf and wonderfully proficient in the handling of the cumbersome craft of his tribe even under the most adverse conditions. At last he succeeded in shoving Nu's boat into the grip of a receding roller that carried it swiftly away from shore, and at the same time he hoved his own through, leaping into it with his captive.

Nat-ul fought her way to her knees, calling aloud to Nu, and striving desperately to throw herself overboard, but Tur held her fast, paddling with one hand, and when Nu reached the water's edge they were well beyond his reach. So, too, was his own tree trunk. Between him and Nat-ul the sea swarmed with carnivorous reptiles. Every instant was carrying her away from him. The troglodyte scarce hesitated. With a swift movement he threw off his lion skin and discarded his stone ax, then, naked but for a loin cloth, and armed only with his knife he dove through the pounding surf into the frightful sea.

As Nat-ul witnessed his act she redoubled her efforts to retard Tur. Crawling to her knees she threw both arms about her captor's neck, dragging him down until he could no longer wield his paddle. Tur fought to disengage himself.

He did not wish to kill or maim his captive – she was far too beautiful to destroy or disfigure – he wanted her in all her physical perfection, just as she was.

Gradually Nu was overhauling them. Twice he was attacked by slimy monsters. Once he fought his way to victory and again the two who menaced him fell to fighting between themselves and forgot their prey. At last he was within reach of Tur's boat. Nat-ul battling with desperation and every ounce of her strength to hamper Tur's movements was tugging at the man's arms. He could do nothing, and already Nu had seized the side of the craft and was raising one leg over it.

With a sudden wrench Tur freed his right hand. Nat-ul strove to regain it, but the great fist rose above her face. With terrific impact it fell upon her forehead. All went black before her as she released her hold upon Tur and sank to the bottom of the boat, unconscious.

Instantly Tur snatched up his paddle and leaping to his feet beat furiously at Nu's head and hands. Bravely the man strove to force his way into the boat in the face of this terrific punishment; but it was too severe, and at last, half stunned, he slipped back into the water, as Tur drove his paddle once again and the rude craft forged away toward the mainland.

When Nat-ul regained consciousness she found herself lying upon a shaggy aurochs' skin beneath a rude shelter of thatch and hide. Her hands and feet were securely bound with tough bullock sinew. When she struggled to free herself they cut into her soft flesh, hurting cruelly. So she lay still looking straight up at the funnel-like peak of the shelter's interior.

She knew where she was. This was one of the strange caves of the people she had seen working upon the tree trunks, for what purpose she now knew. She turned her head toward the entrance. Beyond she saw men and women squatting about small fires, eating. It was already dark. Beyond them were other fires, larger fires that kept the savage carnivora at bay.

And beyond this outer circle of fires, from out of the outer darkness, came the roaring and the coughing, the grunting and the growling of scores of terrible beasts of prey, that slunk back and forth about the encampment thirsting for the blood of the men and women and children who huddled within the safety of the protecting fires.

Occasionally a little boy would snatch up a burning brand and hurl it among the night prowlers. There would be a chorus of angry screams and low toned, rumbling growls as the menacers retreated for an instant, then the ring of shadowy forms, and the glowing spots of burning flame that were their eyes, would reform out of the stygian blackness of the night.

Once a cave-lion, emboldened by familiarity with the camp fires of primitive people, leaped through the encircling ring of flame. Into the midst of a family party he sprang, seizing upon an old man. Instantly a half hundred warriors snatched up their spears, and as the lion turned with his prey and leaped back into the night fifty harpoons caught him in mid-air.

Down he came directly on top of a flaming pile of brush, and with him came the old man. The warriors leaped forward with whirling axes. What mattered it if the old man was pierced by a dozen spears that had been intended for the marauder? They leaped and shouted in savage glee, for the lion was dead even before a single ax had smitten him. The old man was dead, too. Him they hurled out to the beasts beyond the flames; the lion they first skinned.

It was an awful spectacle, that evening scene in the far antiquity of man, when the Boat Builders, come north in search of new fisheries, camped upon the shore of the Restless Sea in the edge of the jungle primeval; but to Nat-ul it presented nothing remarkable. To such scenes she had been accustomed since earliest childhood. Of course, with her people the danger of attack by wild beasts at night was minimized by the fact that her tribe dwelt in caves, the mouths of which could be easily blocked against fourfooted enemies; but she was familiar with the evening fires which burned at the cliff's base while the tribe was gathered to feast or council, and she was used, too, to the sudden charge of some bolder individual amongst the many that always foregathered about the haunts of man at night.

At last the people withdrew to their shelters. Only two girls were left, whose business it was to keep the fire burning brightly. Nat-ul was familiar with this custom and she knew the utilitarian origin of it. Women were the least valuable assets of a tribe. They could best be spared in case of a sudden onslaught by some fierce beast at night – it was the young men, who soon were to become warriors, that must be preserved. The death of a single girl would count for little – her purpose would have been served if the screams of herself and her companion aroused the warriors.

But why not old and useless women instead of young girls? Merely because the instinct of self-preservation is stronger in the young than in the very old. An old woman would have been much less careless of her life than would a young woman, and so might sleep and permit the first to die out – she would have but a few years or months to live anyway and little or nothing to live for in those primitive days.

The young woman, on the contrary, would watch the fires zealously for her own protection, and so insure the greater safety of the tribe. Thus, perhaps, was born the custom from which sprung the order of holy virgins who tended the eternal fires in the temples that were yet unbuilt in the still undreamed-of Rome.

Presently the entrance to the shelter in which Nat-ul was secured was darkened by the figure of a man – it was Tur. Nat-ul recognized him at once. He came to her side and knelt.

'I have kept the women from you,' he said. 'Gron would have torn you to pieces, and the others would have helped her. But you need not fear them. Promise me that you will not resist, or attempt to escape, and you shall be freed from your bonds permanently. Otherwise I shall have to tie you up whenever I am away, and then there is no telling what Gron may do, since you will be defenseless and I not here to keep her from you. What do you say?'

'I say that the moment my hands are freed I shall fight

until I kill or am killed,' replied the girl; 'and when my feet are loosed I shall run away as fast as I can.'

Tur shrugged his shoulders.

'Very well,' he said. 'It will profit you nothing, unless you enjoy being always tied in this uncomfortable position.'

He stooped and commenced to work upon the knots that held her feet and ankles. Outside the shelter something slunk stealthily in the shadows. Tur did not hear the faint scraping sound of the creature's wary advance. His back was toward the entrance of the shelter as he knelt low over the hard knots in the bullock sinews. Already he had released the cords that encircled Nat-ul's ankles, and now he was turning his attention to those at her knees. The girl lay quietly, her face toward the lesser darkness which showed through the entrance. She would wait patiently until he had freed her, and then she would fight until the man was forced to kill her.

Suddenly she became aware of the darker shadow of a form blotting a portion of the dark entrance way. The creature was not large enough to be of the more formidable carnivora, though it might have been a hyena or a wild dog. Nat-ul was on the point of warning the man, when it occurred to her that here might be not only the quick death she now craved, but at the same time a means of revenging herself upon her captor.

She lay very quiet while Tur labored over the last knot. Close behind the man crept the silent prowler of the night. Nat-ul could imagine the bared fangs and the slavering jowls. In another instant there would be a savage growl as the thing closed with a swift spring upon its prey.

Or would it leap past the man upon her unprotected throat? The girl's eyes were wide in fascinated horror. She shuddered once as in the close presence of death. The last knot loosened beneath Tur's fingers. Her jerked the cord from about the girl's knees with a low exclamation of satisfaction.

And then Nat-ul saw the thing behind the man rear upon its hind legs and spring full upon his back. There was no savage growl – no sound. The silence of the attack rendered it infinitely more horrible than would bestial roars and growls that might have proclaimed the nature of the animal.

Tur rolled over upon his side to grapple with his antagonist. In an instant they were locked in furious combat. Nat-ul staggered to her feet. Her arms still were pinioned, but her legs were free. Here was her opportunity! Leaping over the two blood mad beasts she darted from the shelter and plunged into the nearby jungle.

CHAPTER EIGHT

BOUND TO THE STAKE

Nu, the son of Nu, half stunned by the paddle of Tur, still managed to keep afloat until he partially regained his senses. Then, seeing the futility of further attempt to overtake the boat in which Nat-ul was being borne toward the mainland, he struck out for the shore of the island. For a while he lay upon the hot sand, resting. Then he arose looking out across the water. Far in the distance he could see a tiny speck approaching the opposite shore. It must be the boat in which Nat-ul had been carried off. Nu marked the spot – in the distance a lofty mountain peak reared its head far inland.

Nu bethought himself of the boat that had brought him to the island. He looked out to sea for it, but it was not in sight there. He walked along the beach. Beyond a heap of wave washed boulders he came upon the thing he sought. He could have shouted aloud, so elated was he. There before him lay the boat and in it was the paddle. He ran forward and pulled it up upon the beach, then he hurried back to the spot at which he had discarded his robe and ax, and after regaining them returned to the dug-out.

A moment more saw him floundering out through the surf. He leaped into the craft, seized the paddle and struck out for the far off shore line. With paddle and ax and stone knife he fought off the marauders of the sea. The journey was marked by a series of duels and battles that greatly impeded the man's progress. But he was not discouraged. He was accustomed to nothing else. It was his life, as it was the life of every creature that roamed the land or haunted the deeps in those stupendously savage days.

It was quite dark when the heavy booming of the surf before him warned Nu that he was close in-shore. For some time he had seen the fires of the Boat Builders ahead of him and toward these he had directed his way. Now his boat ran its blunt nose out upon the sand a hundred yards north of the camp. Nu leaped out, leaving the boat where it lay. He doubted that he should ever have further use for it, but should he live to return to his people he would lose no time in building a similar craft with which he should fill his father's people with awe and admiration.

About the camp of the Boat Builders, as Nu approached, he discovered the usual cordon of night prowlers that he had naturally expected. Circling until he was down wind from the shelters he was enabled to reach the jungle without being discovered by any of the more ferocious beasts. Once he had just eluded a ponderous cave-bear that was lumbering toward the encampment in search of prey, and again he almost stumbled against a huge rhinoceros as it lay in the long grasses upon the jungle's outer fringe. But once within the jungle he took to the trees, since among their branches there were few that he had reason to fear. The panther sometimes climbed to the lower branches, but, though he was a mighty beast by comparison with the panther of the twentieth century, Nu looked upon him with contempt, since he seldom deliberately hunted man and could be put to flight, if not killed, by a well hurled ax. Reptiles constituted the greatest menace to the jungle traveler who chose the branches of the trees, for here often lurked enormous snakes in whose giant coils the mightiest hunters were helpless as babes.

To the rear of the village Nu traveled through the trees, leaping in the dark from one huge frond to another. When the distance was too great to span in a single leap he came to the ground, springing across the intervening space with the speed and agility of a deer. At last he came to the edge of the jungle opposite the camp. The fires came close beneath the tree in which he hid. He could see the girls tending them, and further in, the balance of the tribe squatting about their smaller cooking fires, gnawing upon bones, or splitting them to extract the marrow.

He saw the rush of the lion upon the opposite side of the camp. He saw him seize the old man. He saw the warriors leap to their feet and run toward the beast. He saw the eyes and attention of every member of the tribe directed toward the spot which was farthest from Nu. Even the girls who were tending the fires below him ran quickly across the village to witness the killing of the marauder.

Taking advantage of this fortuitous good fortune Nu dropped quickly to the ground and ran for the shadows of the shelters which were placed in a rude circle facing outward toward the outer circle of fires with the result that the circular space they enclosed was in partial shadow. Here Nu threw himself upon his belly in the darkest spot he could find. For some time he lay motionless, listening and sniffing the air. As nothing rewarded his observations at this point he rose cautiously upon all fours and crept a few feet further on in the shadows of the shelters. Again he lay down to listen and sniff. For half an hour he pursued his slow way about the inner circle behind the dwellings. The inhabitants had retired – all except the girls who tended the fires.

At last Nu heard low voices coming from the interior of a shelter behind which he had but just crawled. He lay very quiet with his nose a few inches from the bottom of the skin and thatch hut. Presently there came to his sensitive nostrils the evidence he had been seeking – within was Nat-ul; but there was someone with her!

Cautiously Nu crept around to the front of the shelter. Even there it was very dark, for the girls had permitted the fires to die down to a few fitful flames. Opposite the entrance Nu heard Nat-ul's voice distinctly. He saw the form of a man leaning over her. He went hot with hate and rage. Like a beast of prey he slunk noiselessly upon all fours into the shelter directly behind the unsuspecting Tur. Then without a sound he rose to his feet and threw himself full upon the back of the stranger.

His knife was out and his fighting fangs were bared as the two rolled about the floor of the shelter striking, clawing and biting at one another. At last the man raised his voice in a call for help, for Nu was getting the better of him. The long knife had not found a vital spot as yet, for Tur was an experienced fighter and so far had been able to ward off the more dangerous blows; but nevertheless he was bleeding from several wounds and his throat and breast were lacerated by the other's teeth.

In reply to his shouts the village awoke with answering cries. Warriors, bearing their short spears, ran from every shelter. Women and children scampered at their heels. Gron, Tur's mate, was among the first to come. She had recognized the voice of her man and had guessed where he might be in trouble. Like an angry tigress she sprang for the shelter in which the beautiful stranger had been confined. Behind her came the warriors. One carried a burning brand from a nearby fire. He flung it into the interior, careless of where it might land. Fortunately for the inmates it fell beyond them, rolling against the further side of the hut. Instantly the dry fronds of the thatch that had been leaned against the bottom of the skins to fill in the gaps caught fire and the inside of the shelter was illumined by the sudden glare of flames.

When the rescuers saw that but a single man opposed their fellow they threw themselves upon the two, and though Nu battled bravely he was presently overcome. The entire hut was now aflame, so that his captors were forced to drag him outside. Here they bound his arms and legs, and then turned their attention to saving the balance of the village from destruction. This they accomplished by pulling down the blazing shelter with their spears and beating out the flames with fresh hides.

Even in the excitement of the fight Nu had not for a moment forgotten Nat-ul, and when the brand lighted up the interior he had sought for her with his eyes, unsuccessfully – Nat-ul had disappeared.

He wondered what could have become of her. From her

position upon the floor of the hut he had been sure that she was securely bound – otherwise she would have been fighting tooth and nail against her captor. He looked about him from where he lay before the ruins of the burned shelter. He could see nothing of her; but he saw another woman – a young woman with good features but with the expression of a wild beast. Hate, jealousy and rage were mirrored in every line of the passion distorted countenance. It was Gron. She came toward him.

'Who are you?' she cried.

'I am Nu, the son of Nu,' replied the man.

'Are you of the same people as the woman in whose shelter you found my man?' she continued.

Nu nodded affirmatively.

'She was to have been my mate,' he said. 'Where is she?'

For the first time the woman seemed to realize the absence of the fair prisoner. She turned toward Tur.

'Where is the woman?' she shrieked. 'Where have you hidden the woman? No longer shall you keep me from her. This time I shall tear out her heart and drink her blood.'

Tur looked about in consternation.

'Where is the woman?' he called to the warriors; but none seemed to know.

Immediately a search of the village commenced. The warriors ran hither and thither through the huts, and into the enclosure behind them. Nu lay awaiting the outcome of the search. As it became evident that Nat-ul had escaped his heart leaped with joy. At last there was no other place to look and all the searchers had returned – Nat-ul was not in the village.

Gron turned toward Nu.

'Your woman has escaped me,' she shouted; 'but you shall suffer for her,' and she leaped upon him as he lay there bound and defenseless.

In her mad rage she would have torn his eyes out had not a tall warrior interfered. He seized the woman by her hair, jerking her roughly from her victim. Then he swung her, still by the hair, brutally to the ground.

'Take your woman away,' he called to Tur. 'Does a woman rule my people? Take her away and beat her, that she may learn that it is not a woman's place to interfere with the doings of men. Then take you another mate, that this woman may be taught her place.'

Tur seized upon the unfortunate Gron and dragged her toward his own shelter, from which, later, could be heard the sound of a spear haft falling upon flesh, and the shrieks and moans of a woman.

Nu was disgusted. Among his people women were not treated thus. He looked up at the burly form of the chief who was standing over him. Well, why didn't they kill him? That was the proper thing to do with male prisoners. Among his own tribe a spear thrust through the heart would long since have settled the fate of one in Nu's position. He wondered where Nat-ul was. Could she find her way back to the tribe, safely? He wished that he might live but long enough to find her, and see her safe in her father's cave.

The chief was gazing intently upon him; but he had as yet made no move to finish him.

'Who are you?' he at length asked.

'I am Nu, the son of Nu,' replied the prisoner.

'From where do you come?'

Nu nodded toward the north.

'From near the Barren Cliffs,' he replied. 'And should you go thither, beater of women, my father's tribe would fall upon you and kill you all.'

'You talk big,' said the chief.

'I talk truth,' retorted Nu. 'My father's people would laugh at such as you – at men clothed in the skins of cows. It shows what manner of people you be. Now, my father's warriors wear the skins of Ur, and Zor and Oo, and upon their feet are sandals of the hides of Ta and Gluh. They are men. They would laugh as they sent their women and children out with sticks to drive you away.'

This was a terrible insult. The chief of the Boat Builders trembled with rage.

'You shall see,' he cried, 'that we are men. And the manner of your death will prove if you be such a brave man as you say. Tomorrow you shall die – after the day is done and the fires are lighted you shall begin to die; but it will be long before you are dead, and all the time you will be crying out against the woman who bore you, and begging us to put you out of your misery.'

Nu laughed at him. He had heard of distant peoples who tortured their prisoners, and so he guessed what the chief meant to suggest. Well, he would show them how the son of Nu could die.

Presently at the chief's command a couple of warriors dragged Nu into a nearby shelter. A guard was placed before the door, for the escape of Nat-ul had warned them to greater watchfulness.

The long night dragged itself to a slow end. The sun rose out of the Restless Sea. The villagers bestirred themselves. Nu could smell the cooking food. He was very hungry, but they offered him not a single morsel. He was thirsty but none brought him water, and he was too proud to ask favors of his captors.

If the night had been long the day seemed an eternity, and though he knew that darkness was to be the signal for the commencement of the tortures that were to mark his passing he welcomed the first shadows of the declining sun.

Whatever cruelties they might perpetrate upon him could not last forever. Sooner or later he would die, and with this slim comfort Nu, the son of Nu, waited for the end.

The fishers had all returned. The outer ring of fires had been kindled, as well as the smaller cooking fires within. The people squatted about on their haunches gnawing upon their food like beasts. At last they had completed their evening meal. A couple of men brought a small post and after scooping a hole in the ground with their spears set it up halfway between the shelters and the outer fires.

Then two warriors came to the hut where Nu lay. They seized him by the feet and dragged him, upon his back and shoulders, through the village. The women and children poked him with sharp sticks, threw stones at him and spat upon him. Nu, the son of Nu, made no remonstrances. Not by so much as a line did the expression of utter indifference that sat his features like a mask alter in response to painful blows or foul indignities.

At last his guard stopped before the post which was now set firmly upright in the ground. They jerked Nu to his feet, and bound him securely to the stake. In a circle about him was a ring of brush wood. He knew that he was to be slowly roasted, for the brush was nowhere quite close enough for the flames to reach him. It would be a slow death, very pleasant to the eyes of the audience – especially if the victim gave evidence of his agonies. But it was far from the intention of Nu, the son of Nu, to afford the Boat Builders this satisfaction. He looked around upon the ring of eager, savage faces with bored contempt. Nu despised them, not because they would kill him, for that he might expect from any strangers, but because they wore the skins of 'cows' and the men labored instead of devoting all their time and energies to the chase and to warfare.

Their boats were fine to have – Nu had even thought of fashioning one upon his return to his people; but to make a business of such labor – ugh! it was disgusting. Had he escaped he should have returned to the Boat Builders with his father's warriors and taken what boats he wished.

His meditations were cut short by the ceremonies which were going on about him. There had been dancing, and a certain primitive chanting, and now one of the warriors lighted the brush that surrounded the victim at the stake.

CHAPTER NINE

THE FIGHT

After Nu, the son of Nu, had left his father and his father's people to go in search of Nat-ul and Hud, the warrior chief had sat in silence for many minutes. Beside him sat Tha, father of Nat-ul, and round about squatted the other members of the tribe. All were silent in the face of the sorrow that had overtaken their chief and his principal lieutenant. Nu and Nat-ul were great favorites among their savage fellows. Not so, however, Hud, and the anger against him was bitter.

Presently Nu, the chief, spoke.

'We cannot go in search of a new home,' he said, 'leaving two of our children behind.'

His listeners knew that he ignored Hud – that Hud, in bringing this sorrow upon the tribe, had forfeited his rights among them. They were satisfied that it should be so. A young warrior stood up. With his spear he drew a line upon the ground from east to west and lying just north of him.

'Nu, the son of Nu, passed through the ordeals with me – we became men and warriors upon the same day. Together we hunted our first lion.' He paused, and then, pointing to the line he had drawn upon the ground, continued: 'Never shall I cross this line until I have found Nu, the son of Nu.'

As he ceased speaking he drew himself to his full height and with arms folded across his broad chest turned to face his chief.

From the tribe came grunts of approval. All eyes turned toward Nu. What would he do? The young warrior's act was nothing short of rebellion. Suddenly Aht, brother of Nat-ul, sprang to his feet and stood beside the defiant warrior. He said nothing – his act proclaimed his intention.

Nu, the chief, looked at the two young men from beneath his shaggy brows. The watchers were almost certain that a half smile played grimly about his grim countenance. He, too, arose. He walked to where the two stood and ranged himself beside them.

Tha was the first to guess the significance of the act, and the instant that he did so he leaped to Nu's side. Then the others understood, and a moment later the whole tribe was ranged with their backs to Dag's line, facing toward the south. They were dancing and shouting now. The men waved their stone axes or threw their long spears high in air. The women beat their palms together, and the little children ran skipping about, getting in everyone's way.

After a few minutes of this Nu started off toward the

south, telling off a score of men to remain with the women and children who were to follow slowly back toward their former dwellings while the chief with the balance of the fighting men searched rapidly ahead for signs of Nu and Nat-ul.

First they came upon the dead body of Hud within the cave in the face of the Barren Cliffs. From there they discovered Nu's spoor and faint traces of the older spoor of the girl, showing that Nu had not overtaken her at this point.

On they went along the beach toward their old caves, and everywhere the signs of one or the other of those they followed were distinguishable. It was dark when they reached the caves, and the following morning they had difficulty in again picking up the spoor because of the fact that the tide had obliterated it where it had touched the sandy beach at low tide. Now Nu separated his warriors into three parties. One, with which he remained, was to keep south along the beach, the second was to work into the jungle for a mile and then turn south, while the third was to search straight inland toward the west. In this way one of them must come upon those they sought, or some sign of them.

Tha was in command of the central party, and Aht was with him. Dag was with Nu, the chief. They beat rapidly along the beach, and spread out across it from the water to the jungle, that nothing might escape their observation.

Several times they followed false leads into the jungle, so that they lost much time, with the result that darkness came upon them without their having discovered the two they sought.

They camped upon the sand just outside the jungle, building a ring of fires about them to keep off the wild beasts. Then they lay down to sleep – all but two who kept watch and tended the fires.

Dag was one of the watchers. As the night grew darker he became aware of a glow in the south. He called his companion's attention to it.

'There are men there,' he said. 'That is the light from beast-fires. Listen!'

Savage yells rose faintly from the distance, and in the direction of the lights. Dag was on the point of arousing Nu when his keen eyes detected something moving warily between the jungle and the camp. Evidently it had but just crept out of the dense vegetation. Ordinarily Dag might have thought it a beast of prey; but with the discovery of the nearness of a camp of men, he was not so sure.

True, men seldom crept through the jungle after darkness had fallen; but there was something about the movements of this creature that suggested the crawling of a man on all fours.

Dag circled the camp, apparently oblivious of the presence of the intruder. He threw a stick upon a blaze here, and there he stamped out some smoking faggots that had fallen inside the ring. But all the while he watched the movements of the thing that crept through the outer darkness toward the camp.

He could see it more distinctly now, and was aware that from time to time it cast a backward glance over its shoulder.

'Had it a companion, or companions? Was something following it?' Dag scrutinized the black face of the jungle beyond the creeping thing.

'Ah! so that was it?'

A dark shadow had stepped from the somber wood upon the trail of the creature that was now halfway across the open space between the jungle and the camp. Dag needed no second glance to attest the identity of the newcomer. The lithe body, the black mass that marked the bristling mane, the crouching pose, the two angry spotches of yellow green fire – no doubt here. It was Zor, the lion, stalking his prey.

Dag whispered a word to his companion who came to his side. The two stood looking straight toward the nearer creature, with no attempt to disguise the fact that they had discovered it.

'It is a man,' whispered Dag's companion.

And then, with a frightful roar, Zor charged, and the creature before it rose upon two feet full in the light of the nearer blaze. With a cry that aroused the whole camp Dag leaped beyond the flaming circle, his spear hand back thrown, the stone head, laboriously chipped to a sharp point, directed at the charging Zor.

The weapon passed scarce a hand's breadth from the shoulder of Zor's prey and buried itself in the breast of the beast. At the same instant Dag leaped past the fugitive, placing himself directly in the path of the lion with only an ax and knife of stone to combat the fury of the raging, wounded demon of destruction.

Over his shoulder he threw a word to the one he had leaped forth to succor.

'Run within the beast-fires, Nat-ul,' he cried; 'Zor's mate is coming to his aid.'

And sure enough, springing lightly across the sands came a fierce lioness, maned like her lord.

Now Dag's fellow warrior had sprung to his side, and from the camp were running the balance of the savage spearmen. Zor, rearing upon his hind feet, was striking at Dag who leaped nimbly from side to side, dodging the terrific blows of the mighty, taloned paws, and striking the beast's head repeatedly with his heavy ax.

The other warrior met the charge of the infuriated lioness with his spear. Straight into the broad breast ran the sharp point, the while the man clung tenaciously to the haft, whipped hither and thither as the beast reared and wheeled and struck at him with her claws.

Now Nu, the chief, and his fellows arrived upon the scene. A score of spears bristled from the bodies of Zor and his mate. Axes fell upon their heads, and Nu, the mighty, leaped upon Zor's back with only his stone knife. There he clung to the thick mane, driving the puny weapon time and again into back and side until at last the roaring, screaming beast rolled over upon its side to rise no more.

The lioness proved more tenacious of life than her lord, and though bristling with spears and cut to ribbons with the knives of her antagonists she charged into close quarters with a sudden rush that found one of the cave men a fraction of a second too slow. The strong claws raked him from neck to groin and as he fell the mighty jaws closed with a sickening crunch upon his skull.

At bay over her victim the lioness stood growling and threatening, while the wild warriors danced in a circle about her awaiting the chance to rush in and avenge their comrade.

Within the circle of fires Nat-ul replenished the blaze, keeping the whole scene brilliantly lighted for the warriors. That she had stumbled upon men of her own tribe so unexpectedly seemed little short of miraculous. She could scarce wait for the battle with the lions to be concluded, so urgent was the business that filled her thoughts.

But at last Zor's savage mate lay dead, and as Nu, the chief, returned to the camp Nat-ul leaped forward to meet him.

'Quick!' she cried. 'They are killing Nu, thy son,' and she pointed toward the south in the direction of the glare that was now plainly visible through the darkness.

Nu did not wait to ask questions then. He called his warriors about him.

'Nat-ul says that they slay Nu, the son of Nu, there,' he said, pointing toward the distant fire-glow. 'Come!'

As Nat-ul led them along the beach and through the jungle she told Nu, the chief, all that had transpired since Hud had stolen her away. She told of her wanderings, and of the Boat Builders. Of how one had chased her, and of the terrible creature that had seized and carried her to its nest. She told of the strange creature that crawled into the shelter where she was confined, leaping upon the back of Tur. And of how she slipped out of the shelter as the two battled, and escaped into the jungle, wriggling her hands from their bonds as she ran. She shuddered as she told Nu of the gauntlet of savage beasts she had been forced to run between the beast-fires of the Boat Builders and the safety of the jungle trees.

'I rested for the balance of the night in a great tree close beside the village of the strangers,' she said. 'Early the next morning I set out in search of food, intending to travel northward until I came to our old dwelling where I could live in comparative safety.

'But all the time I kept wondering what it might have been that leaped upon Tur's back in the shelter the night before and the more I thought about it the more apparent it became that it might have been a man – that it it must have been a man, for what animal could pass through the beast-fires unseen?

'And so, after filling my stomach, I crept back through the trees to the edge of the village, and there I watched. The sun then was straight above me – half the day was gone. I could not reach the caves before darkness if anything occurred to delay me, and as I might at any moment stumble upon some of the strangers or be treed by Ur, or Zor, or Oo, I decided to wait until early tomorrow morning before setting out for the caves. There was something within me that urged me to remain. What it was I do not know; but it was as though there were two Nat-uls, one wishing to hurry away from the land of the strangers as rapidly as possible and the other insisting that it was her duty to remain. At last I could deny my other self no longer – I must stay, and so I found a comfortable position in a great tree that grows close beside the clearing where the strangers' village stands, and there I remained until long after darkness came.

'It was then that I saw the thing within the village that sent me here. Before, I had seen your fires, and wondered who it might be that came from the north. I knew that all the strangers had returned in the afternoon, so it could be none of them, and the first tribe to the north I knew was my own, so I hoped, without believing, that it might indeed be some of thy warriors, Nu.

'And then I saw that something was going to occur in the village below me. Warriors approached a hut from which they dragged a captive. By the legs they dragged him, through the village and about it, and as they did so the women and children tortured and spat upon the prisoner.

At first I could not see the victim plainly, but at last as they raised him to his feet and bound him to a stake where they are going to roast him alive among slow fires I saw his face.

'Oh, Nu, can you not guess who it was that had followed me so far, had overcome such dangers and fought his way through the awful waters to rescue me?'

'Nu, the son of Nu,' said the old warrior, and his chest swelled with pride as he strode through the jungle in the rear of the village.

Angry beasts of prey menaced the rescuing party upon every hand. Twice were they attacked and compelled to battle with some fierce, primordial brute; but at last they won to the edge of the jungle behind the village they sought.

There the sight that met their eyes and ears was one of wild confusion. Men and women were running hither and thither uttering shouts of rage. Beyond them was a circle of flaming brush. In the center of this, Nat-ul told the rescuers, Nu, the son of Nu, was fast bound to a stake. Slowly he was roasting to death – possibly he was already dead.

Nu gathered his warriors about him. Two he commanded to remain always beside Nat-ul. Then, with the others at his heels, his long, white feather nodding bravely above his noble head, and the shaggy pelt of Ur, the cave bear, falling from his shoulders, Nu, the chief, slunk silently out of the jungle toward the village of the excited Boat Builders.

There were forty of them, mighty men, mightily muscled. In their strong hands they grasped their formidable spears and heavy axes. In their loin cloths rested their stone knives for the moment when they closed in hand-to-hand combat with foes. In their savage brains was but a single idea – to kill – to kill – to kill!

To the outer rim of fires they came and yet the excited populace within had not discovered them. Then a girl, remembering tardily her duties at the fires, turned to throw more brush upon the blaze and saw them – saw a score of handsome, savage faces just beyond the flames.

With a scream of terror and warning she turned and scurried amongst the villagers. For an instant the hub-hub was stilled, only to break out anew at the girl's frightened cry of: 'Warriors! Warriors!'

Then Nu and his men were among them. The warriors of the Boat Builders ran forward to meet the attackers. The women and children fled to the opposite side of the enclosure. Hoarse shouts and battle cries rang out as the Cliff Dwellers hurled themselves upon the Boat Builders. A shower of long slim spears volleyed from one side, to be answered by the short, stout harpoons of the villagers.

Then the warriors rushed to closer conflict with their axes. Never after the first assault was the outcome of the battle in question – the fiercer tribe of Nu – the hunters of beasts of prey – the warrior people – were the masters at every turn. Back, back they forced the wearers of 'cow' skins, until the defenders had been driven across the enclosure upon their women and children.

And now the inner circle of fires was surrendered to the invaders, and as Nat-ul sprang between the warriors of her people to be first to the side of Nu and cut away his bonds, the last of the Boat Builders turned and fled into the outer darkness, along the beach to where their boats were drawn up beyond the tide.

Nu, the chief, leaped through the flames upon the heels of Nat-ul. In the terrible heat within the two came side by side before the stake. The girl gave a single glance at the bare and smoking pole and at the ground around it before she turned and threw herself into Nu's arms.

Nu, the son of Nu, was not there, nor was his body within the enclosure.

CHAPTER TEN

GRON'S REVENGE

Gron, suffering and exhausted from the effects of the cruel beating Tur had administered, lay all the following day in her shelter. Tur did not molest her further. Apparently he had forgotten her, a suggestion which aroused all her primitive savagery and jealousy as no amount of brutal punishment might have done.

All day she lay suffering, and hating Tur. All day she planned new and diabolical schemes for revenge. Close to her breast she hugged her stone knife. It was well for Tur that he did not chance to venture near her then. While he had beaten her the knife had remained in her loin cloth, nor had the thought to use it against her mate entered the head of Gron; but now, now that he had deserted her, now that he was doubtless thinking upon a new mate her thoughts constantly reverted to the weapon.

It was not until after nightfall that Gron crawled from beneath the hides and thatch of her shelter. She had not eaten for twenty-four hours, yet she felt no hunger – every other sense and emotion was paralyzed by the poison of jealousy and hate. Gron slunk about the outskirts of the crowd that pressed around the figure at the stake.

Ah, they were about to torture the prisoner! What pleasure they would derive from that! Gron raised herself on tip-toe to look over the shoulder of a woman. The latter turned, and, recognizing her, grinned.

'Tur will enjoy the death agonies of the mate of the woman he is going to take in your stead, Gron,' taunted her friend.

Gron made no reply. It was not the way of her period to betray the emotions of the heart. She would rather have died than let this woman knew that she suffered.

'That is why he was so angry,' continued the tormentor, 'when you tried to rob him of this pleasure.'

With the woman's words a sudden inspiration flashed into the mind of Gron. Yes, Tur would be made mad if the prisoner escaped. So would Scarb, the chief who had commanded Tur to beat her and to take another mate.

Gron raised herself again upon her toes and looked long and earnestly at the face of the man bound to the stake. Already the flames of the encircling fires illuminated his figure and his every feature – they stood out as distinctly as by sunlight. The man was very handsome. There was no man among the tribe of Scarb who could compare with the stranger in physical perfection and beauty. A gleam of pleasure shot Gron's dark eyes. If she could only find such another man, and run off with him then, indeed, would she be revenged upon Tur. If it could be this very man! Ah, then, indeed, would Scarb and Tur both be punished. But that, of course, was impossible – the man would be dead in a few hours.

Gron wandered about the village – too filled with her hate to remain long in one place. Like an angry tigress she paced to and fro. Now and again some other woman of the tribe hurled a taunt or a reproach at her.

It would be ever thus. How she hated them – every one of them. As she passed her shelter in her restless rounds she heard the plaintive wailing of her child. She had almost forgotten him. She hurried within, snatching up the infant from where it lay upon a pile of otter and fox skins.

This was Tur's child – his man-child. Already it commenced to resemble the father. How proud Tur was of it. Gron gasped at the hideous thought that followed remorselessly upon the heels of this recollection. She held the child at arm's length and tried to scrutinize its features in the dim interior of the hut.

How Tur would suffer if harm befell his first man-child – his only offspring! Gron almost threw the wee bundle of humanity back upon its pile of skins, and leaping to her feet ran from the shelter.

For half an hour she roamed restlessly about the camp. Her brain was a whirling chaos of conflicting emotions. A dozen times she approached the death fires that were slowly roasting alive the man bound to the stake they encircled. As yet they had not injured him – but given him a taste of the suffering to come, that was all.

Suddenly she came face to face with Tur. Involuntarily her hands went out in a gesture of appeal and supplication. She was directly in Tur's path. The man stopped and looked at her for an instant, then with a sneer that was half snarl he raised his hand and struck her in the face.

'Get out of my way, woman!' he growled, and passed on.

A group of women, standing near, had seen. They laughed boisterously at the discomfiture of their sister. But let us not judge them too harshly – it was to require countless ages of humanizing culture before their sisters yet unborn were to be able to hide the same emotions.

Gron went cold and hot and cold again. She burned with

rage and humiliation. She froze with resolve – a horrid resolve. And suddenly she went mad. Wheeling from where she stood she ran to the shelter that housed her babe. In the darkness she found the wee thing. It was Tur's. Tur loved it. For a moment she pressed the soft cheek to her own, she strained the warm body close to her breasts. Then – May God forgive her, for she was only a wild thing goaded to desperation.

Dropping the pitiful bundle to the floor of the shelter Gron ran back into the open. She was wild eyed and disheveled. Her long black hair streamed about her face and across her shoulders. She ran to the outskirts of the crowd that was watching the victim who obstinately refused to gratify their appetite for human suffering – Nu would not wince. Already the heat of the flames must have caused him excruciating agony, yet not by the movement of a muscle did he admit knowledge of either the surrounding fires or the savage, eager spectators.

Gron watched him for a moment. His fate was to be hers when Tur and Scarb discovered the deed she had committed, for a man-child was a sacred thing.

And now there sprang to Gron's mind a recurrence of the thought that the taunting female's words had implanted there earlier in the evening. How could she compass this last stroke of revenge? It seemed practically impossible. The stake was hemmed in upon all sides by the clustering horde of eager tribesmen.

Gron turned and ran to the opposite side of the village, beyond the shelters. There was no one there. Even the girls tending the fires had deserted their posts to witness the last agonies of the prisoner. Gron seized a leafy branch that lay among the firewood that was to replenish the blaze. With it she beat out two of the fires, leaving an open avenue into the enclosure through which savage beasts might reasonably be expected to venture. Then she ran back to the crowding ring of watchers.

As she approached them she cried out in apparently incoherent terror. Those nearest her turned, startled by her shrieks.

'Zors!' she cried. 'The fires have died and four of them have entered the shelters where they are devouring the babes. On that side,' and she pointed to the opposite side of the enclosure.

Instantly the whole tribe rushed toward the ring of huts. First the warriors, then the women and children. The victim at the stake was deserted. Scarce was every back turned toward the prisoner than Gron leaped through the fiery girdle to his side.

Nu saw the woman and recognized her. He saw the knife in her hand. She had tried to kill him the previous night, and now she was going to have her way. Well, it was better than the slow death by fire.

But Gron's knife did not touch Nu. Instead it cut quickly through the bullock sinews that bound him to the stake. As the last strand parted the woman seized him by the hand.

'Come!' she cried. 'Quick, before they return – there are no Zors in the village.'

Nu did not pause to question her, or her motives. For a few steps he staggered drunkenly, for the bonds had stopped the circulation in his arms and legs. But Gron, half supporting, half dragging him, pulled him across the fires about the stake, on past the outer circle of the beast-fires toward the Stygian blackness that enveloped the beach toward the sea.

As Nu advanced the blood commenced to circulate once more through the veins from which it had been choked, so that by the time they came to the water he was almost in perfect command of his muscles.

Here Gron led him to a dug-out.

'Quick!' she urged, as the two seized it to run it through the surf. 'They will soon be upon us and then we shall both die.'

Already angry shouts were plainly distinguishable from the village, and the firelight disclosed the tribe running hither and thither about the fires that encircled the stake to which Nu had been secured. The boat was through the surf and riding the waves beyond. Gron had clambered in and Nu was taking his place in the opposite end of the craft, when a new note arose from the village. The savage shouting carried a different tone. Now there were battle cries where before there had been but howls of rage. Even at the distance at which they were Gron and Nu could see that a battle was raging among the shelters of the Boat Builders. What could it mean?

'They have fallen upon one another,' said Gron. 'And while they fight let us hasten to put as great a distance between them and ourselves as we can before the day returns.'

But Nu was not so anxious to leave. He wanted to know more of the cause of the battle. It was not within the bounds of reason that the villagers could have set upon one another with such apparent unanimity, and without any seeming provocation, and, too, it appeared to Nu that there were more people in the village now than there had been before he left it. What did all this mean? Why, it meant to the troglodyte that the village had been attacked by enemies, and he wished to wait until he might discover the identity of the invaders.

But Gron did not wish to wait. She seized her paddle and commenced to ply it.

'Wait!' urged Nu, but the woman insisted that they must hasten or be lost.

Even as they argued Gron suddenly leaned forward pointing toward the beach.

'See!' she whispered. 'They have discovered us. We are being pursued.'

Nu looked in the direction that she pointed, and, sure enough, dimly through the night he described two forms racing toward the beach. As he looked he saw them seize upon a boat and start launching it, and then he knew that only in immediate flight lay safety. He seized his paddle and in concert with Gron struck out for the open sea.

'We can turn to one side presently and elude them,' whispered the woman.

Nu nodded.

'We will turn north toward my country,' he said.

Gron did not demur. She might as well go north as south. Her life was spent. There was to be no more happiness for her. Her thoughts haunted the dim interior of a hide shelter where lay a pathetic bundle upon a pile of fox and otter skins.

For a while both were silent, paddling out away from shore. Behind them they now and then discerned the darker blotch of the pursuing canoe upon the dark waters of the sea.

'Why did you save me?' asked Nu, at length.

'Because I hated Tur,' replied the woman.

Nu fell silent, thinking. But he was not thinking of Gron. His mind was filled with speculations as to the fate of Nat-ul. Whither had she fled when she had escaped from the clutches of the Boat Builders? Could she have reached the tribe in safety? Had she known that it was Nu who had entered the shelter where she lay and rescued her from Tur? He thought not, for had she known it he was sure that she would have remained and fought with him.

Presently Gron interrupted his reveries. She was pointing over the stern of the boat. There, not fifty yards away, Nu saw the outlines of another craft with two paddlers within.

'Hasten!' whispered Gron. 'They are overtaking us, and but for my knife we are unarmed.'

Nu bent to his paddle. On the boat wallowed toward the open sea. There was no chance to elude the pursuers and turn north. First they must put sufficient distance between them that the others might not see which way they turned. But there seemed little likelihood of their being able to accomplish this for, strive as they would, they could not shake off the silent twain.

The darkest hours of the night were upon them – those that precede dawn. They struggled to outdistance their pursuers. That they were lengthening the distance between the two boats seemed certain. In another few minutes they might risk the stratagem. But they had scarcely more than turned when the surge of surf upon a beach rose directly before them. Both were nonplussed. What had happened? Where were they? They had been moving straight out to sea for some time, and yet there could be no mistaking that familiar sound – land was directly ahead of them. To turn back now would mean to run straight into the arms of their pursuers – which neither had the slightest desire to do. Had

Nu been armed he would not have hesitated to grapple with the two occupants of the boat that had clung so tenaciously to their wake, but with only the woman's knife and a couple of wooden paddles it would have been a fruitless thing to do.

Exerting all their strength the two drove the dug-out through the surf until its nose ran upon the sand. Then they leaped out and dragged the boat still further up beyond the reach of the mightiest roller.

Where were they? Nu guessed a part of the truth. He reasoned that they had fallen upon the same island from which he had seen Nat-ul snatched by the Boat Builder, and from which he himself had escaped so recently.

But he was not quite right. Their strenuous paddling during the hours of darkness had carried them to the north of the nearer island and beyond it. As a matter of fact they had been deposited upon the southern coast of the largest island of the group which lay several miles northeast of the one with which Nu had had acquaintance.

But what mattered it? One was as bad as another. Both belonged to the Mysterious Country. They were inhabited by hideous flying reptiles, and legend held that frightful men dwelt upon them. And Nu was without weapons of defense!

Who of us has not dreamed of going abroad upon the public streets in scant attire or in no attire whatever? What painful emotions we have suffered! Yet how insignificant our plight by comparison with that of the primeval troglodyte thrown into a strange country without his weapons – without even a knife!

Nu was lost, but far from hopeless. He did not turn to the woman with the question: 'What shall we do now?' If primeval man was anything he was self-reliant. Heredity, environment and all of Nature's mightiest laws combined to make him so. Otherwise he would have perished off the face of the earth long before he had had an opportunity to transmit his image to posterity – there would have been no posterity for him. Some other form than ours would have exhumed his bones from the drift of the ages and wondered upon the structure and habits of the extinct monstrosity whose hinder limbs were so much longer than his fore limbs that locomotion must have been a tiresome and painful process interrupted by many disastrous tumbles upon the prehistoric countenance.

But Nu, the son of Nu, was not of a race doomed to extinction. He knew when to fight and when to flee. At present there was nothing to flee from, but a place of safe hiding must be their first concern. He grasped Gron by the wrist.

'Come!' he said. 'We must find a cave or a tree to preserve us until the day comes again.'

The woman cast a backward glance over her shoulder – a way with women.

'Look!' she whispered, and pointed toward the surf.

Nu looked, and there upon the crest of a great wave, outlined against the dark horizon, loomed a boat in which sat two figures, plying paddles. One glance was enough. The pursuers were close upon them. Nu, still holding Gron's wrist, started toward the black shadows above the beach. The woman ran swiftly by his side.

Nu wondered not a little that the woman should thus flee her own people to save him, a stranger and an enemy. Again he raised the question that Gron had so illy answered.

'Why do you seek to save me,' he asked, 'from your own people?'

'I do not seek to save you,' replied the woman. 'I wish to make Tur mad – that is all. He will think I have run off to mate with you. When he thinks that, you may die, for all that I care. I hate you, but not quite so much as I hate Tur.'

CHAPTER ELEVEN

THE AUROCHS

As Nu led Gron through the dark night amidst the blackness of the tropical forest that clothed the gentle ascent leading inland from the beach he grinned at the thought of Tur's discomfiture, as well as the candor of his rescuer.

But now Nu was the protector. He might have left the woman to shift for herself. She had made it quite plain that she had no love for him – as plain as words could convey the idea: 'I hate you, but not quite so much as I hate Tur.' But the idea of deserting Gron never occurred to him. She was a woman. She had saved Nu's life. Her motive was of negligible import.

In the darkness Nu found a large tree. He entered the lower branches to reconnoiter. There were no dangerous foes lurking there, so he reached down and assisted Gron to his side. There they must make the best of it until daylight returned – it would never do to roam through the woods unarmed at night longer than was absolutely necessary.

Nu was accustomed to sleeping in trees. His people often did so when on the march, or when the quarry of the chase led them overfar from their caves by day, necessitating the spending of the night abroad; but Gron was not so familiar with life arboreal. She clung, fearful, to the bole of the tree in a position that precluded sleep.

Nu showed her how to compose herself upon a limb with her back to the tree stem, but even then she was afraid of falling should she chance to doze. At last Nu placed an arm about her to support her, and thus she slept, her head pillowed upon the shoulder of her enemy.

The sun was high when the sleepers awoke. Gron was the first to open her eyes. For a moment she was bewildered by the strangeness of her surroundings. Where was she? Upon what was her head pillowed? She raised her eyes. They fell upon the sun-tanned, regular features of the god-like Nu. Slowly recollection forced its way through the misty pall of somnolence. She felt the arm of the man about her, still firmly flexed in protective support.

This was her enemy – the enemy of her people. She looked at Nu through new eyes. It was as though the awakening day had brought an awakening of her soul. The man was undeniably beautiful – of a masculine beauty that was all strength. Gron closed her eyes again dreamily and let her head sink closer to the strong, brown shoulder. But presently came entire wakefulness, and with it a full return of actively functioning recollection. She saw the pitiful bundle lying among the fox and otter skins upon the floor of the distant shelter.

With a sudden intaking of her breath that was almost a scream, Gron sat erect. The movement awakened Nu. He opened his eyes, looked at the woman, and removing his arm from about her stood upright upon the tree branch.

'First we must seek food and weapons,' he said, 'and then return to the land that holds my country. Come.'

His quick eyes had scanned the ground below. There were no beasts of prey in sight. Nu lowered the woman to the base of the tree, leaping lightly to her side. Fruits, growing in plenitude, assauged the keenest pangs of hunger. This accomplished, Nu led the way inland toward higher ground where he might find growing the harder wood necessary for a spear shaft. A fire-hardened point was the best that he might hope for temporarily unless chance should direct him upon a fragment of leek-green nephrite, or a piece of flint.

Onward and upward toiled the searchers, but though they scaled the low and rugged mountains that paralleled the coast they came upon neither the straight hard wood that Nu sought, nor any sign of the prized minerals from which he might fashion a spear head, an ax, or a knife.

Down the further slopes of the mountains they made their way, glimpsing at times through the break of a gorge a forest in a valley far below. Toward this Nu bent his steps. There might grow the wood he sought. At last they reached the last steep declivity, a sheer drop of two hundred feet to the leveler slopes whereon the forest grew almost to the base of the cliff.

For a moment the two stood gazing out over the unfamiliar scene – a rather open woodland that seemed to fringe the shoulder of a plateau, dropping from sight a mile or so beyond them into an invisible valley above which hung a soft, warm haze. Far beyond all this, dimly rose the outlines of far-off mountains, their serrated crests seemingly floating upon the haze that obscured their bases.

'Let us descend,' said Nu, and started to lower his legs over the edge of the precipice.

Gron drew back with a little exclamation of terror.

'You will fall!' she cried. 'Let us search out an easier way.'

Nu looked up and laughed.

'What could be easier than this?' he asked.

Gron peered over the edge. She saw the face of a rocky wall, broken here and there by protruding boulders, and again by narrow ledges where a harder stratum had better withstood the ravages of the elements. In occasional spots where lodgment had been afforded lay accumulations of loose rock, ready to trip the unwary foot, and below all a tumbled mass of jagged pieces waiting to receive the bruised and mangled body of whomever might be so foolhardy as to choose this way to the forest. Nu saw that Gron was but little reassured by her inspection.

'Come!' he said. 'There is no danger – with me.'

Gron looked at him, conscious of an admiration for his courage and prowess – an admiration for an enemy that she would rather not have felt. Yet she did feel the truth of his words: 'There is no danger – with me.' She sat down upon the edge of the cliff, letting her legs dangle over the abyss. Nu reached up and grasped her arm, drawing her down to his side. How he clung there she could not guess, but somehow, as he supported her in the descent, he found handholds and stepping stones that made the path seem a miracle of ease. Long before they reached the bottom Gron ceased to be afraid and even found herself discovering ledges and outcroppings that made the journey easier for them both. And when they stood safely amid the clutter of debris at the base she threw a glance of ill concealed admiration upon her enemy. Mentally she compared him with Tur and Scarb and the other males of the Boat Builders, nor would the comparison have swelled the manly chests of the latter could they have had knowledge of it.

'Those who follow us will stop here,' she said, 'nor do I see any break in the cliff as far as my eye can travel,' and she looked to right and left along the rocky escarpment.

'I had forgotten that we might be followed,' said Nu; 'but when we have found wherewith to fashion a spear and an ax, let them come – Nu, the son of Nu, will welcome them.'

From the base of the cliff they crossed the rubble and stepped out into the grassy clearing that reached to the forest's edge. They had crossed but halfway to the wood when they heard the crashing of great bodies ahead of them, and as they paused the head of a bull aurochs appeared among the trees before them. Another and another came into sight, and as the animals saw the couple they halted, the bulls bellowing, the cows peering wide eyed across the shaggy backs of their lords.

Here was meat and only the knife of the woman to bring it down. Nu reached for Gron's weapon.

'Go back to the cliff,' he said, 'lest they charge. I will bring down a young she.'

Gron was about to turn back as Nu had bid her, and the man was on the point of circling toward the right when there appeared on either side of the aurochs several men. They were clothed in the skins of the species they accompanied, and were armed with spears and axes. At sight of Nu and Gron they raised a great shout and dashed forward toward the two. Nu, unarmed, perceived the futility of accepting battle. Instead he grasped Gron's hand and with her fled back toward the cliffs. Close upon their heels came the herders, shouting savage cries of carnage and victory. They had their quarry cornered. The cliff would stop them, and then, with their backs against the wall, the man would be quickly killed and the woman captured.

But these were not cliff dwellers – they knew nothing of the agility of Nu. Otherwise they would not have slowed up, as they did, nor spread out to right and left for the purpose of preventing a flank escape by the fugitives. Across the rubble ran Nu and Gron, and at the foot of the cliff where they should have stopped, according to the reasoning of the herders, they did not even hesitate. Straight up the sheer wall sprang Nu, dragging the woman after him. Now the aurochs' herders raised a mighty shout of anger and dismay. Who had ever seen such a thing! It was impossible, and yet there before their very eyes they beheld a man, encumbered by a woman, scaling the unscalable heights.

With renewed speed the herders dashed straight toward

the foot of the cliff, but Nu and Gron were beyond the reach of their hands before ever they arrived. Turning for an instant, Nu saw they were not yet out of reach of the weapons. He reached down with his right hand and picked up a loose bit of rock, hurling it toward the nearest spearman. The missile struck its target full upon the forehead, crumpling him to an inert mass.

Then Nu scrambled upward again, and before the herders could recover from their surprise he had dragged Gron out of range of the spears. Squatting upon a narrow ledge, the woman at his side, Nu hurled insulting epithets at their pursuers. These he punctuated with well-timed and equally well-aimed rocks, until the yelling herders were glad to retreat to a safer distance.

The enemy did not even venture the attempt to follow the fugitives. It was evident that they were no better climbers than Gron. Nu held them in supreme contempt. Had he but a good ax he would descend and annihilate the whole crew!

Gron, sitting close beside Nu, was filled with wonder and something more than wonder that this enemy should have risked so much to save her, for at the bottom of the cliff Nu had evidently forgotten for the instant that the woman was not of his own breed, able to climb equally as well as he, and had ascended a short distance before he had discovered that Gron was scrambling futilely for a foothold at the bottom. Then, in the face of the advancing foemen, he had descended to her side, risking capture and death in the act, and had hoisted her to a point of safety far up the cliff face. Tur would never have done so much.

The woman, stealing stealthy glances at the profile of the young giant beside her, felt her sentiments undergoing a strange metamorphosis. Nu was no longer her enemy. He protected her, and now she looked to him for protection with greater assurance of receiving it than ever she had looked to Tur for the same thing. She knew that Nu would forage for her – upon him she depended for food as well as protection. She had never looked for more from her mate. Her mate! She stole another half shy glance at Nu. Ah, what a mate he would have been! And why not? They were alone in the world, separated from their people, doubtless forever. Gron suddenly realized that she hoped that it was forever. She wondered what was passing in Nu's mind.

Apparently the man was wholly occupied with the joys of insulting the threatening savages beneath him; but yet his thoughts were busy with plans for escape. And why? Solely because he yearned for his own land and his father's people? Far from it. Nu might have been happy upon this island forever had there been another there in place of Gron. He thought of Nat-ul – no other woman occupied his mind, and his plans for escape were solely a means for returning to the mainland and again taking up his search for the daughter of Tha.

For an hour the herders remained in the clearing near the foot of the cliff, then, evidently tiring of the fruitless sport, they collected their scattered herd and disappeared in the wood toward the direction from which they had come. A half hour later Nu ventured down. He had discovered a cave in the face of the cliff and there he left Gron, telling her that he would fetch food to her, since in case of pursuit he could escape more easily alone than when burdened with her.

After a short absence he returned with both food and drink, the latter carried in the bladder that always hung from his gee-string. He had seen nothing of the herders and naught of the hard wood or the materials for spear and ax heads that he had desired.

'There is an easier way, however,' he confided to the woman, as they squatted at the mouth of the cave and ate. 'The drivers of aurochs bore spears and axes and knives. It will be easier to follow them and take theirs than to make weapons of my own. Stay here, Gron, in safety, and Nu will follow the strangers, returning shortly with weapons and the flesh of the fattest of the she aurochs. Then we will return to the coast, fearless of enemies, find the boat and go back to Nu's country. There you will be well received, for Nu, my father, is chief, and when he learns that you have saved my life he will treat you well.'

So Nu dropped quickly down to the foot of the cliff,

crossed the clearing, and a moment later disappeared from the eyes of Gron into the shadows of the wood.

For a while he could make neither head nor tail to the tangled spoor of the herd, but at last he found the point where the herders evidently had collected their charges and driven them in a more or less compact formation toward the opposite side of the forest. Nu went warily, keeping every sense alert against surprise by savage beast or man. Every living thing that he might encounter could be nothing other than an enemy. He stopped often, listening and sniffing the air. Twice he was compelled to take to the trees upon the approach of wandering beasts of prey; but when they had passed on Nu descended and resumed his trailing.

The trampled path of the herd led to the further edge of the forest, and there Nu saw unfolded below him as beautiful a scene as had ever broken upon his vision. The western sun hung low over a broad valley that stretched below him, for the wood ended upon the brow of a gentle slope that dropped downward to a blue lake sparkling in the midst of green meadows a couple of miles away.

Upon the surface of the lake, apparently floating, were a score or more strange structures. That they were man-built Nu was certain, though he never had seen or dreamed of their like. To himself he thought of them as 'caves', just as he had mentally described the shelters of the Boat Builders, for to Nu any human habitation was a 'cave', and that they were the dwellings of men he had no doubt since he could see human figures passing back and forth along the narrow causeways that connected the thatched structures with the shore of the lake. Across these long bridges they were driving aurochs, too, evidently to pen them safely for the night against the night prowlers of the forest and the plain.

Until darkness settled Nu watched with unflagging interest the activities of the floating village. Then in the comparative safety of the darkness he crept down close to the water's edge. He took advantage of every tree and bush, of every rock and hollow that intervened between himself and the enemy to shelter and hide his advance. At last he lay concealed in a heavy growth of reeds upon the bank of the lake. By separating them before his eyes he could obtain an excellent view of the village without himself being discovered. The moon had risen, brilliantly flooding the unusual scene. Now Nu saw that the dwellings did not really float upon the surface. He discovered the ends of piles that disappeared beneath the surface of the water. The habitations stood upon these. He saw men and women and little children gathered upon the open platforms that encircled many of the structures, and upon the narrow bridges that spanned the water between the dwellings and the shore. Fires burned before many of the huts, blazing upon little hearths of clay that protected the planking beneath them from combustion. Nu could smell the savory aroma of cooking fish, and his mouth watered as he saw the teeth of the Lake Dwellers close upon juicy aurochs' steaks, while others opened shellfish and devoured their contents raw, throwing the shells into the water below them.

But, hungry though he was for meat, the objects of his particular desire were the long spear, the heavy ax and the sharp knife of the hairy giant standing guard upon the nearest causeway. Upon him Nu's eyes rested the oftenest. He saw the villagers, the evening meal consumed and the scraps tossed into the water beneath their dwellings, engaged in noisy gossip about their fires. Children romped and tumbled perilously close to the edges of the platforms. Youths and maidens strolled to the darker corners of the village, and leaning over the low rails above the water conversed in whispers. Loud voiced warriors recounted for the thousandth time the details of past valorous deeds. The younger mothers, in little circles, gossiped with much nodding of heads, the while they suckled their babes. The old women, toothless and white-haired, but still erect and agile in token of the rigid primitive laws which governed the survival of the fit alone, busied themselves with the care of the older children and various phases of the simple household economy which devolved upon them.

The evening drew on into darkness. The children had been posted off to their skin covered, grass pallets. For another half hour the elders remained about the fires, then, by twos and threes, they also sought the interiors of the huts, and sleep. Quiet settled upon the village, and still Nu, hidden in the reeds beside the lake, watched the nearest guardsman. Now and then the fellow would leave his post to replenish a watch fire that blazed close to the shore end of his causeway. Past this no ordinary beast of prey would dare venture, nor could any do so without detection, for its light illumined brightly the end of the narrow bridge.

Nu found himself wondering how he was to reach the sentry unseen. To rush past the watch fire would have been madness, for the guard then would have ample time to raise an alarm that would call forth the entire population of the village before ever Nu could reach the fellow's side.

There was the water, of course, but even there there was an excellent chance of detection, since upon the mirrorlike surface of the moonlit lake the swimmer would be all too apparent from the village. A shadow fell directly along the side of the causeway. Could he reach that he might make his way to a point near the sentry and then clamber to close quarters before the man realized that a foe was upon him. However, the chance was slight at best, and so Nu waited hoping for some fortuitious circumstance to offer him a happier solution of his problem.

As a matter of fact he rather shrank from the unknown dangers of the strange waters in which might lurk countless creatures of destruction; but there was that brewing close at hand that was to force a decision quickly upon the troglodyte, leaving but an immediate choice between two horns of a dilemma, one carrying a known death and the other a precarious problematical fate.

It was Nu's quick ears that first detected the stealthy movement in the reeds behind him, down wind, where his scent must have been carrying tidings of his presence to whatever roamed abroad in that locality. Now the passing of a great beast of prey upon its way through the grasses or the jungle is almost noiseless, and more so are his stealthy footfalls when he stalks his quarry. You or I could not detect them with our dull ears amid the myriad sounds of a primeval night – the coughing and the moaning of the great cats punctuated by deafening roars, the lowing and bellowing and grunting of the herds – the shrill scream of pain and terror as a hunter lands upon the neck or rump of his prey – the hum of insects – the hissing of reptiles – the rustling and soughing of the night wind among the grasses and the trees. But Nu's ears were not as ours. Not only had he been aware of the passing and repassing of great beasts through the reeds behind him, but, so quick his perceptive faculties, he immediately caught the change from mere careless passage to that of stealthy stalking on the part of the creature in his rear. The beast had caught his scent and now, cautiously, he was moving straight toward the watcher upon the shore.

Nu did not need the evidence of his eyes to picture the great pads carefully raised and cautiously placed so that not a bent grass might give out its faint alarm, the lowered and flattened head, the forward tilted ears, the gentle undulations of the swaying tail, lashing a little at the tufted tip. He saw it all, realizing too all that it meant to him. There was no escape to right or left, and before him lay the waters of the unknown lake. He was all unarmed, and the mighty cat was now almost within its leap.

Nu looked toward the sentry. The fellow had just returned from replenishing his watch fire. He stood leaning over the railing gazing into the water. What was that? Nu's eyes strained through the darkness toward the platform where the warrior stood. Just behind him was another figure. Ah! the figure of a woman. Stealthily, with many a backward glance, she approached the sentinel. There was a low word. The man turned, and at sight of the figure so close beside him now he opened his arms and crushed the woman to him.

Her face was buried on his shoulder, his head turned from Nu and doubtless his eyes hidden in the red-brown hair that fell, unconfined, almost to the woman's waist.

And then the great carnivore at Nu's back sprang.

CHAPTER TWELVE

TUR'S DECEPTION

At the instant that the beast leaped for him Nu dove forward into the lake. The water was shallow, not over two or three feet deep, but the cave man hugged the bottom, worming his way to the left toward the shadows of the causeway. He knew that the cat would not follow him into the lake – his greatest danger now lay in the unknown denizens of the water. But, though every instant he expected to feel a slimy body or sharp teeth, he met with no attack.

At last, his breath spent, he turned upon his back, floating until his nose and mouth rose above the surface. Filling his lungs with air he sank again and continued his way in the direction of the piling. After what seemed an eternity to him his hand came at last in contact with the rough surface of a pile. Immediately he rose to the surface, and to his delight found that he was beneath the causeway, safe from the eyes of the guardsman and his companion.

Upon the bank behind him he could hear the angry complaining of the baffled cat. He wondered if the noise of his escape had alarmed the sentry to greater watchfulness. For long he listened for some sign from above, and at last he caught the low tones of whispered conversation. Good! they were still at their lovemaking, with never a thought for the dangers lying close at hand.

Nu wished that they would be done. He dared not venture aloft while the woman was there. For an hour he waited waist deep in water, until finally he heard her retreating footsteps above him. He gave her time to regain her dwelling, and then with the agility of a cat he clambered up the slippery pile until his fingers closed upon the edge of the flooring of the causeway. Cautiously he drew himself up so that his eyes topped the upper surface of the platform.

A dozen paces from him was the sentry moving slowly shoreward toward the watchfire. The man's back was toward Nu, and he was already between Nu and the shore. Nothing could have been better.

The cave man crawled quickly to the platform, and with silent feet ran lightly in the wake of the guard. The man was beside the pile of wood with which he kept up the fire and was bending over to gather up an armful when Nu overtook him. With the speed and directness of a killing lion Nu leaped full upon his quarry's back. Both hands sought the man's throat to shut off his cries for help, and the teeth of the attacker buried themselves in the muscles behind the collar bone that he might not easily be shaken from his advantageous hold.

The sentry, taken entirely by surprise by this attack from the rear, struggled to turn upon his foe. He tore at the fingers at his throat that he might release them for the little instant that would be sufficient for him to call for help; but the viselike grip would not loosen. Then the victim groped with his right hand for his knife. Nu had been expecting this, and waiting for it. Instantly his own right hand released its grip upon the other's throat, and lightning-like followed the dagger hand in quest of the coveted blade, so that Nu's fingers closed about those of the sentry the instant that the latter gripped the handle of the knife.

Now the blade flew from its sheath drawn by the power of two hands, and then commenced a test of strength that was to decide the outcome of the battle. The Lake Dweller sought to drive the knife backward into the body of the man upon his back. Nu sought to force the knife hand upward and outward. The blade was turned backward. Nu did not attempt to alter this – it was as he would have it. Slowly his mighty muscles prevailed over those of his antagonist, and still his left hand choked off the other's voice. Upward, slowly but surely, Nu carried the knife hand of his foe. Now it is breast high, now to the other's shoulder, and all the time the hairy giant is attempting to drive it back into the body of the cave man.

At the instant that it rose level with the sentry's shoulder

Nu pushed the hand gradually toward the left until the blade hovered directly over the heart of its owner. And then, quite suddenly, Nu reversed the direction of his exertions, and like lightning the blade, driven by the combined strength of both men, and guided by Nu, plunged into the heart of the Lake Dweller.

Silently the man crumpled beneath the weight upon him. There was a final struggle, and then he lay still. Nu did not wait longer than to transfer all the coveted weapons from the corpse of his antagonist to his own body, and then, silent and swift as a wraith, he vanished into the darkness toward the forest and the heights above the lake.

Gron, alone in the cave, sat buried in thought. Sometimes she was goaded to despair by recollections of her lost babe, and again she rose to heights of righteous anger at thoughts of the brutality and injustice of Tur. Her fingers twitched to be at the brute's throat. She compared him time and time again with Nu, and at each comparison she realized more and more fully the intensity of her new found passion for the stranger. She loved this alien warrior with a fierceness that almost hurt. She relived again and again the countless little episodes in which he had shown her a kindness and consideration to which she was not accustomed. Among her own people these things would have seemed a sign of weakness upon the part of a man, but Gron knew that no taint of weakness lay behind that noble exterior.

For long into the night she sat straining her eyes and ears through the darkness for the first intimation of his return. At last, when he had not come, she commenced to feel apprehension. He had gone out unarmed through the savage land to wrest weapons from the enemy. Already he might be dead, yet Gron could not believe that aught could overcome that mighty physique.

Toward morning she became hopeless, and crawling within the cave curled up upon the grasses that Nu had gathered for her, and slept. It was several hours after dawn when she was awakened by a sound from without – it was the scraping of a spear butt against the rocky face of the cliff, as it trailed along in the wake of a climbing man.

As Gron saw who it was that came she gave a little cry of joy, braving the dangers of the perilous declivity to meet him. Nu looked up with a smile, exhibiting his captured weapons as he came. He noted the changed expression upon the woman's face – a smile of welcome that rendered her countenance quite radiant. He had never before taken the time to appraise Gron's personal appearance, and now it was with a sense of surprise that was almost a shock that he realized that the woman was both young and goodlooking. But this surprise was as nothing by comparison with that which followed, for no sooner had Gron reached him than she threw both arms about his neck, and before he realized her intent had dragged his lips to hers.

Nu disengaged himself with a laugh. He did not love Gron – his heart was wholly Nat-ul's, and his whole mind now was occupied with plans for returning to his own country where he might continue his search for her who was to have been his mate. Still laughing, and with an arm about Gron to support her up the steep cliff, he turned his steps toward the cave.

'I have brought a little food,' he said, 'and after I have slept we will return to the sea. On the way I can hunt, for now I have weapons, but in the meantime I must sleep, for I am exhausted. While I sleep you must watch.'

But once within the cave Gron, carried away by her new found love, renewed her protestations of affection; but even with her arms about him Nu saw only the lovely vision of another face – his Nat-ul. Where was she?

When Nat-ul and Nu, the chief, discovered that the son of Nu no longer was bound to the flame-girt stake in the village of the Boat Builders they turned toward one another in questioning surprise. The man examined the stake more closely.

'It is not burned,' he said, 'so, therefore, Nu could not have been burned. And here,' he pointed at the ground about the stake, 'look, here are the cords that bound him.'

He picked one of them up, examining it.

'They have been cut! Some one came before us and liberated Nu, the son of Nu.'

'Who could it have been, and whither have they gone?' questioned Nat-ul.

Nu shook his head. 'I do not know, and now I may not stop to learn, for my warriors are pursuing the strangers and I must be with them,' and Nu, the chief, leaped across the dying fires after the yelling spearmen who chased the enemy toward the sea.

But Nat-ul was determined to let nothing stay her search for Nu, the son of Nu. Scarcely had the young man's father left her than she turned back toward the shelters. First she would search the village, and if she did not find him there she would go out into the jungle and along the beach – he could not be far. As Nat-ul searched the shelters of the Boat Builders, a figure hid beneath a pile of aurochs' skins in one of them, stirred, uncovered an ear, and listened. The sounds of conflict had retreated, the village seemed deserted. An arm threw aside the coverings and a man sprang quickly to his feet. It was Tur. Hard pressed by the savage spearmen of the caves and surrounded, the man had crawled within a hut and hidden himself beneath the skins.

Now he thought he saw a chance to escape while the enemy were pursuing his people. He approached the entrance to the shelter and peered out. Quickly he drew back – he had seen a figure emerging from the next hut. It was a woman, and she was coming toward the shelter in which he had concealed himself. The light of the beast-fires played upon her. Tur drew in his breath in pleased surprise – it was the woman he had once captured and who had escaped him.

Nat-ul advanced rapidly to the shelter. She thought them all deserted. As she entered this one she saw the figure of a man dimly visible in the darkness of the interior. She thought it one of the warriors of her own tribe, looting. Oftentimes they could not wait the total destruction of an enemy before searching greedily for booty.

'Who are you?' she asked, and then, not waiting for an answer: 'I am searching for Nu, the son of Nu.'

Tur saw his opportunity and was quick to grasp it.

‘I know where he is,’ he said. ‘I am one of Scarb’s people, but I will lead you to Nu, the son of Nu, if you will promise that you will protect me from your warriors when we return. My people have fled, and I may never hope to reach them again unless you promise to aid me.’

Nat-ul thought this a natural and fair proposition, and was quick to accept it.

‘Then come,’ cried Tur. ‘There is no time to be lost. The man is hidden in a cove south of here along the shore. He is fast bound and so was left without a guard. If we hurry we may reach him before my people regain him. If we can elude your warriors and the delay that would follow their discovery of me we may yet be in time.’

Tur hurried from the shelter followed by Nat-ul. The man was careful to keep his face averted from the girl while they traversed the area lit by the camp and beast-fires, so he forged ahead trusting to her desire to find her man to urge her after him. Nor did he over-estimate the girl’s anxiety to find Nu, the son of Nu. Nat-ul followed swiftly upon Tur’s heels through the deserted village and across the beach from whence the sounds of conflict rose beside the sea.

Tur kept to the north of the fighters, going to a spot upon the beach where he had left his own boat. He found the craft without difficulty, pushed it into the water, lifted Nat-ul into it, and shoved it through the surf. To Tur the work required but a moment – he was as much at home in the boiling surf as upon dry land.

Seated in the stern with Nat-ul facing him in the bow he forced the dug-out beyond the grip of the rollers. Nat-ul took up a second paddle that lay at her feet, plying it awkwardly perhaps, but not without good effect. She could scarce wait until the boat reached the cove, and every effort of her own added so much to the speed of the craft.

Tur kept the boat’s head toward the open sea. It was his purpose to turn toward the south after they were well out, and, moving slowly during the night, await the breaking dawn to disclose the whereabouts of his fellows. That they, too, would paddle slowly southward he was sure.

Presently he caught sight of the outline of a boat just

ahead. Probably beyond that were others. He had been fortunate to stumble upon the last boat-load of his fleeing tribe. He did not hail them for two reasons. One was that he did not wish the girl to know that he was not bearing her south toward the cove – the imaginary location of her man; and the other was due to the danger of attracting the attention of the boats and be carrying the pursuit out upon the sea.

Presently a third possibility kept him quiet – the boat ahead might contain warriors of the enemy searching for fugitives. Tur did not know that the tribe of Nu was entirely unfamiliar with navigation – that never before had they dreamed of such a thing as a boat.

So Tur followed the boat ahead in silence straight out to sea. To Nat-ul it seemed that the cove must be a long distance away. In the darkness she did not perceive that they were traveling directly away from shore. After a long time she heard the pounding of surf to the left of the boat. She was startled and confused. Traveling south, as she supposed they had been doing, the surf should have been off the right side of the boat.

'Where are we?' she asked. 'There is land upon the left, whereas it should be upon the right.'

Tur laughed.

'We must be lost,' he said; but Nat-ul knew now that she had been deceived. At the same instant there came over her a sudden sense of familiarity in the voice of her companion. Where had she heard it before? She strove to pierce the darkness that shrouded the features of the man at the opposite end of the boat.

'Who are you?' she asked. 'Where are you taking me?'

'You will soon be with your man,' replied Tur, but there was an ill-concealed note of gloating that did not escape Nat-ul.

The girl now remained silent. She no longer paddled, but sat listening to the booming of the surf which she realized that they were approaching. What shore was it? Her mind was working rapidly. She was accustomed to depending largely on a well developed instinct for locality and direction upon land, and while it did not aid her much upon the water it at least preserved her from the hopeless bewilderment that besets the average modern when once he loses his bearings, preventing any semblance of rational thought in the establishment of his whereabouts. Nat-ul knew that they had not turned toward the north once after they had left the shore, and so she knew that the mainland could not be upon their left. Therefore the surf upon that hand must be breaking upon the shore of one of the islands that she only too well knew lay off the mainland. Which of the islands they were approaching she could not guess, but any one of them was sufficiently horrible in her estimation.

Nat-ul planned quickly against the emergency which confronted her. She knew, or thought, that the man had brought her here where she would be utterly helpless in his power. Her people could not follow them. There would be none to succor or avenge.

Tur was wielding his paddle rapidly and vigorously now. He shot the boat just ahead of an enormous roller that presently caught and lifted it upon its crest carrying it swiftly up the beach. As the keel touched the sand Tur leaped out and dragged the craft as far up as he could while the wave receded to the ocean.

Nat-ul stepped out upon the beach. In her hand she still held the paddle. Tur came toward her. He was quite close, so close that even in the darkness of the night she saw his features, and recognized them. He reached toward her arm to seize her.

'Come,' he said. 'Come to your mate.'

Like a flash the crude, heavy paddle flew back over Nat-ul's shoulder, cleaving the air downward toward the man's head. Tur, realizing his danger, leaped back, but the point of the blade struck his forehead a glancing blow. The man reeled drunkenly for a second, stumbled forward and fell full upon his face on the wet sand. The instant that the blade touched her tormentor Nat-ul dropped the paddle, dodged past the man, and scurried like a frightened deer toward the black shadows of the jungle above the beach.

The next great roller washed in across the prostrate form of Tur. It rolled him over, and as it raced back toward the sea it dragged him with it; but the water revived him, and he came coughing and struggling to his hands and knees, clinging desperately to life until the waters receded, leaving him in momentary safety. Slowly he staggered to his feet and made his way up the beach beyond the reach of the greedy seas.

His head hurt him terribly. Blood trickled down his cheek and clotted upon his hairy breast. And he was mad with rage and the lust for vengeance. Could he have laid his hands upon Nat-ul then she would have died beneath his choking fingers. But he did not lay hands upon her, for Nat-ul was already safely ensconced in a tree just within the shadows of the jungle. Until daylight she was as safe there from Tur as though a thousand miles separated them. A half hour later Nu and Gron, a mile further inland, were clambering into another tree. Ah, if Nat-ul could but have known it, what doubt, despair and suffering she might have been spared.

Tur ran down the beach in the direction in which he thought that he heard the sound of the fleeing Nat-ul. Yes, there she was! Tur redoubled his speed. His quarry was just beneath a tree at the edge of the jungle. The man leaped forward with an exclamation of savage satisfaction – that died upon his lips, frozen by the horrid roar of a lion. Tur turned and fled. The thing he had thought was Nat-ul proved to be a huge cave lion standing over the corpse of its kill. Fortunate for Tur was it that the beast already had its supper before it. It did not pursue the frightened man, and so Tur reached the safety of a nearby tree, where he crouched, shaking and trembling, throughout the balance of the night. Tur was a boat builder and a fisherman – he was not of the stock of Nu and Nat-ul – the hunters of savage beasts, the precursors of warrior nations yet unborn.

CHAPTER THIRTEEN

NAT-UL IS HEART-BROKEN

It was late in the morning when Nat-ul awoke. She peered through the foliage in every direction but could see no sign of Tur. Cautiously she descended to the ground. Upon the beach, not far separated, she saw two boats. To whom could the other belong? Naturally, to some of the Boat Builders. Then there were other enemies upon the island beside Tur. She looked up and down the beach. There was no sign of man or beast. If she could but reach the boats she could push them both through the surf, and, someway, dragging one, paddle the other away from the island. This would leave no means of pursuit to her enemies. That she could reach the mainland she had not the slightest doubt, so self-reliant had heredity and environment made her.

Again she glanced up and down the beach. Then she raced swiftly toward the nearest boat. She tugged and pushed upon the heavy thing, until at last, after what seemed to her anxious mind many minutes she felt it slipping loose from its moorings of sand. Slowly, inch by inch, she was forcing it toward the point where the rollers would at last reach and float it. She had almost gained success with this first boat when something impelled her to glance up. Instantly her dream of escape faded, for from up the beach she saw Tur running swiftly toward her. Even could she have managed to launch this one boat and enter it, Tur easily could overtake her in the other. The water was his element – hers was the land, the caves and the jungles.

Abandoning her efforts with the boat she turned and fled back toward the jungle. A couple of hundred yards behind her raced Tur, but the girl knew that once she reached the tangled vegetation of the forest it would take a better man than Tur to catch her. Straight into the mazes of the wood she plunged, sometimes keeping to the ground and again running through the lower branches of the trees.

All day she fled scarce halting for food or drink, for several times from the elevation of the foot hills and the mountains that she traversed after leaving the jungle she saw the man sticking to her trail. It was dark when she came at last to a precipitous gulf, dropping how far she could not guess. Below and as far as her eyes could reach all was impenetrable darkness. About her, beasts wandered restlessly in search of prey. She caught their scent and heard their dismal moaning, or the thunder of their titanic roaring.

That the cliff upon the verge of which she had halted just in time to avert a plunge into its unknown depths was a high one she was sure from the volume of night noises that came up to her from below, mellowed by distance. What should she do? The summit of the escarpment was nude of trees insofar as she could judge in the darkness, at least she had not recently passed through any sort of forest.

To sleep in the open would be dangerous in the extreme, probably fatal. To risk the descent of an unknown precipice at night might prove equally as calamitous. Nat-ul crouched upon the brink of the abyss at a loss as to her future steps. She was alone, a woman, practically unarmed, in a strange and savage land. Hope that she might ever return to her own people seemed futile. How, indeed, could she accomplish it, followed by enemies and surrounded by unknown dangers.

She was very hungry and thirsty and sleepy. She would have given almost her last chance for succor to have lain down and slept. She would risk it. Drawing her shaggy robe about her, Nat-ul stretched herself upon the hard earth at the top of the precipice. She closed her eyes, and sleep would have instantly claimed her had not a stealthy noise not a dozen yards behind her caused her to come to startled wakefulness. Something was creeping upon her – death, in some form, she was positive. Even now she heard the heavy breathing of a large animal, and although the wind was blowing between them she caught the pungent odor of a great cat.

There was but a single alternative to remaining and surrendering herself to the claws and fangs of the carnivore, nor did Nat-ul hesitate in accepting it. With the speed of a swift she lowered herself over the edge of the cliff, her feet dangling in space. Rapidly, and yet without panic, she groped with her feet for a hold upon the rocky surface below her.

There seemed nothing, not the slightest protuberance that would give her a chance to lower herself from the clutches of the beast that she knew must be sneaking cautiously toward her from above. A sudden chill of horror swept over her as she felt hot breath and the drip of saliva upon her hands where they clung to the edge of the cliff above.

A low growl came from above. Evidently the beast was puzzled by the strange position of its quarry, but in another moment it would seize her wrists or, reaching down, bury its talons in her head or back. And just then her fingers slipped from their hold and Nat-ul dropped into the darkness.

That she fell but a couple of feet did not detract an iota from the fright she endured in the instant that her handhold gave way, but the relief of feeling a narrow ledge beneath her feet quickly overcame her terror. That the beast might follow her she had little fear. There might be a ledge running down to this point, and then again there might not. All she could do was stay where she was and hope for the best, and so she settled herself as securely as she might to await what the immediate future might hold for her. She heard the beast growling angrily as it paced along the brow of the cliff above her, now stopping occasionally to lower its nose over the edge and sniff at her, and again reaching down a mighty paw whose great talons clawed desperately to seize her, sweeping but a few inches above her head.

For an hour or more this lasted until the hungry cat, baffled and disgruntled, wandered away into the jungle in search of other prey, voicing his anger as he went in deep throated roars.

Nat-ul felt along the ledge to right and left with her fingers. The surface of the rock was weatherworn but not polished as would have been true were the ledge the accustomed pathway of padded feet. The girl felt a sense of relief in this discovery – at least she was not upon the well beaten trail leading to the lair of some wild beast, or connecting the cliff top with the valley below.

Slowly and cautiously she wormed her way along the ledge, searching for a wider and more comfortable projection, but the ledge only narrowed as she proceeded. Having ventured thus far the girl decided to prosecute her search until she discovered a spot where she might sleep in comparative safety and comfort. As no such place seemed to exist at the level at which she was, she determined to descend a way. She lowered her feet over the ledge, groping with her sandaled toes along the rough surface below her. Finally she found a safe projection to which she descended. For half an hour Nat-ul searched through the pitch black night upon the steep cliff-face until accident led her groping feet to the mouth of a cave – a darker blot upon the darkness of the cliff. For a moment she listened attentively at the somber opening. No sound of breathing within came to her keen ears. Satisfied that the cave was untenanted Nat-ul crawled boldly in and lay down to sleep – exhausted by her long day of flight.

A scraping sound upon the cliff face awakened Nat-ul. She raised herself upon an elbow and listened attentively. What was it that could make that particular noise? It did not require but an instant for her to recognize it – a sound familiar since infancy to the cliff dweller. It was the trailing of the butt of a spear as it dangled from its rawhide thong down the back of a climbing warrior. Now it scraped along a comparatively smooth surface, now it bumped and pounded over a series of projections. What new menace did it spell?

Nat-ul crawled cautiously to the opening of the cave. Here she could obtain a view of the cliff to the right, but the climber she could not see – he was below the projecting ledge that ran before the threshold of her cavern. As she looked Nat-ul was startled to see a woman emerge from a cave a trifle above her and fifty feet, perhaps, to her right. The watcher drew back, lest she be discovered. She heard the stranger's cry of delight as she sighted the climber below.

She saw her clamber down to meet the new comer. She saw the man an instant later as he clambered to the level of her ledge. Her heart gave a throb of happiness – her lips formed a beloved name; but her happiness was short lived, the name died ere ever it was uttered. The man was Nu, the son of Nu, and the woman who met him threw her arms about his neck and covered his lips with kisses. It was Gron. Nat-ul recognized her now. Then she shrank back from the sight, covering her eyes with her hands, while hot tears trickled between her slim, brown fingers. She did not see Nu's easy indifferent laugh as he slipped Gron's arms from about his neck. Fate was unkind, hiding this and unsealing Nat-ul's eyes again only in time to show the distracted girl a momentary glance of her lover disappearing into Gron's cave with an arm about the woman's waist.

Nat-ul sprang to her feet. Tears of rage, jealousy and mortification blinded her eyes. She seized the knife that lay in her girdle. Murder flamed hot in her wild, young heart as she stepped boldly out upon the ledge. She took a few hurried steps in the direction of the cave which held Nu and Gron. To the very threshold she went, and then, of a sudden, she paused. Some new emotion seized her. A flood of hot tears welled once more to her eyes – tears of anguish and hurt love this time.

She tried to force herself within the cave, but pride held her back. Then sorrowfully she turned away and descended the cliff face. As she went her speed increased until by the time she reached the level before the forest she was flying like a deer from the scene of her greatest sorrow. On through the woods she ran, heedless of every menace that might lurk within its wild shadows. Beyond the wood she came upon a little plain that seemed to end at the edge of a declivity some distance ahead of her. Beyond, in the far distance she could see the tops of mountains rising through a mist that floated over an intervening valley.

She would keep on. She cared not what lay ahead, only that at each step she was putting a greater distance between herself and the faithless Nu, the hateful Gron. That was all that counted – to get away where none might ever find her –

to court death – to welcome the end that one need never seek for long in that savage, primeval world.

She had crossed half the clearing, perhaps, when the head of a bull aurochs appeared topping the crest of the gulf ahead. The brute paused to look at the woman. He lowered his head and bellowed. Directly behind him appeared another and another. Ordinarily the aurochs was a harmless beast, fighting only when forced to it in self-defense; but an occasional bull there was that developed bellicose tendencies that made discretion upon the side of an unarmed human the better part of valor. Nat-ul paused, measuring the distance between herself and the bull and herself and the nearest tree.

While Nat-ul, torn by anguish, fled the cliff that sheltered Nu, the man, within the cave with Gron, again disengaged the fingers of the woman from about his neck.

'Cease thy love-making, Gron,' he said. 'There may be no love between us. In the tribe of Nu, my father, a man takes but one mate. I would take Nat-ul, the daughter of Tha. You are already mated to Tur. You have told me this, and I have seen his child suckling your breast. I love only Nat-ul – you should love only Tur.'

The woman interrupted him with an angry stamp of her sandaled foot.

'I hate him,' she cried. 'I hate him. I love only Nu, the son of Nu.'

The man shook his head, and when he spoke it was still in a kindly voice, for he felt only sorrow for the unhappy woman.

'It is useless, Gron,' he said, 'for us to speak further upon this matter. Together we must remain until we have come back to our own countries. But there must be no love, nor more words of love between us. Do you understand?'

The woman looked at him for a moment. What the emotion that stirred her heart her face did not betray. It might have been the anger of a woman scorned, or the sorrow of a breaking heart. She took a step toward him, paused, and then throwing her arms before her face turned and sank to the floor of the cave, sobbing.

Nu turned away and stepped out upon the ledge before the cave. His quick eyes scanned the panorama spread out before him in a single glance. They stopped instantly upon a tiny figure showing across the forest in the little plain that ran to the edge of the plateau before it dove into the valley beside the inland sea. It was the figure of a woman. She was running swiftly toward the declivity. Nu puckered his brows. There was something familiar about the graceful swing of the tiny figure, the twinkling of the little feet as they raced across the grassy plain. Who could it be? What member of his tribe could have come to this distant island? It was but an accidental similarity, of course; but yet how wildly his heart beat at the sight of the distant figure! Could it be? By a remote possibility could Nat-ul have reached this strange country?

Coming over the edge of the plateau from the valley beyond, Nu saw the leaders of a herd of aurochs. Behind these must be the herders. Will the girl be able to escape them? Ah, she has seen the beasts – she has stopped and is looking about for a tree, Nu reasoned, for women are oft-times afraid of these shaggy bulls. He remembered, with pride, that his Nat-ul feared little or nothing upon the face of the earth. She was cautious, of course, else she would not have suvived a fortnight. Feared nothing! Nu smiled. There were two things that filled Nat-ul with terror – mice and earthquakes.

Now Nu sees the first of the herders upon the flanks of the herd. They are hurrying forward, spears ready, to ascertain what it is that has brought the leaders to a halt – what is causing the old king-bull to bellow and paw the earth. Will the girl see them? Can she escape them? They see her now, and at the same instant it is evident that she sees them. Is she of their people? If so, she will hasten toward them. No! She has turned and is running swiftly back toward the forest. The herders spring into swift pursuit. Nu trembled in excitement. If he only knew. If he only knew!

At his shoulder stood Gron. He had not been aware of her presence. The woman's eyes strained across the distance to the little figure racing over the clearing toward the forest.

Her hands were tightly clenched against her breast. She too, had been struck with the same fear that haunted Nu. Perhaps she had received the idea telepathically from the man.

The watchers saw the herders overtake the fugitive, seize her and drag her back toward the edge of the plateau. The herd was turned back and a moment later all disappeared over the brink. Nu wavered in indecision. He knew that the captive could not be Nat-ul, and yet something urged him on to her succor. They were taking her back to the Lake Dwellings! Should he follow? It would be foolish – and yet suppose that it *should* be Nat-ul. Without a backward glance the man started down the cliff-face. The woman behind him, reading his intention plainly, took a step after him, her arms outstretched toward him.

'Nu!' she cried. Her voice was low and pleading. The man did not turn. He had no ears, no thoughts beyond the fear and hope that followed the lithe figure of the captive girl into the hidden valley toward the distant lake.

Gron threw out her arms toward him in a gesture of supplication. For a moment she stood thus, motionless. Nu continued his descent of the cliff. He reached the bottom and started off at a rapid trot toward the forest. Gron clapped her open palm across her eyes, and, turning, staggered back to the ledge before the cave, where, with a stifled moan she sank to her knees and slipped prone upon the narrow platform.

CHAPTER FOURTEEN

'I HAVE COME TO SAVE YOU'

Nu reached the edge of the plateau in time to see the herders and their captive arrive at the dwellings on the lake. He saw the crowds of excited natives that ran out to meet them. He saw the captive pulled and hauled hither and thither. The herders pointed often toward the plateau behind them. It was evident that Nu's assault upon the sentry of the previous night taken with the capture of this stranger and the appearance of Nu and Gron upon the cliff the day before had filled the villagers with fear of an invasion from the south. This only could account for the early return of the herders with their aurochs.

Taking advantage of what cover the descent to the valley afforded and the bushes and trees that dotted the valley itself, Nu crept cautiously onward toward the lake. He was determined to discover the identity of the prisoner, though even yet he could not believe that she was Nat-ul. A mile from the shore he was compelled to hide until dark, for there was less shelter thereafter and, too, there were many of the natives moving to and fro, having their herds browsing in the bottom lands close to their dwellings.

When it was sufficiently dark Nu crept closer. Again he hid in the reeds, but this time much closer to one of the causeways. He wished that he knew in precisely which of the dwellings the captive was confined. He knew that it would be madness to attempt to search the entire village, and yet he saw no other way.

At last the villagers had retired, with the exception of the sentries that guarded the narrow bridges connecting the dwellings with the shore. Nu crept silently beneath the nearest causeway. Wading through the shallow water he made his way to a point beyond the sentinel's post. Then he crossed beneath the dwelling until he had come to the opposite side. Here the water was almost to his neck. He climbed slowly up one of the piles. Stopping often to listen, he came at last to a height which enabled him to grasp the edge of the flooring above with the fingers of one hand. Then he drew himself up until his eyes topped the platform. Utter silence reigned about him – utter silence and complete darkness. He raised himself, grasping the railing, until one knee rested upon the flooring, then he drew himself up, threw a leg over the railing and was crouching close in the shadows against the wall.

Here he listened intently for several minutes. From within

came the sound of the heavy breathing of many sleepers. Above his head was an opening – a window. Nu raised himself until he could peer within. All was darkness. He sniffed in the vain hope of detecting the familiar scent of Nat-ul, but if she were there all sign of her must have been submerged in the sweaty exhalations from the close packed men, women and children and the strong stench of the illy cured aurochs hides upon which they slept.

There was but one way to assure himself definitely – he must enter the dwelling. With the stealth of a cat he crawled through the small aperture. The floor was almost covered with sleepers. Among them, and over them Nu picked his careful way. He bent low toward each one using his sensitive nostrils in the blind search where his eyes were of no avail. He had crossed the room and assured himself that Nat-ul was not there when a man appeared in the doorway. It was the sentry. Nu flattened himself against the wall not two yards from the door. What had called the fellow within? Had he been alarmed by the movement within the hut? Nu waited with ready knife. The man stepped just within the doorway.

'Throk!' he called. One of the sleepers stirred and sat up.

'Huh?' grunted he.

'Come and watch – it is your turn,' replied the sentry.

'Ugh,' replied the sleepy one, and the sentry turned and left the hut.

Nu could hear him who had been called Throk rising and collecting his weapons, donning his sandals, straightening and tightening his loin cloth. He was making ready for his turn at sentry duty. As he listened a bold scheme flashed into Nu's mind. He grasped his knife more tightly, and of a sudden stepped boldly across the room toward Throk.

'Sh!' he whispered. 'I will stand watch in your place tonight, Throk.'

'Huh?' questioned the sleepy man.

'I will stand watch for you,' repeated Nu. 'I would meet—' and he mumbled a name that might have been anything, 'she said that she would come to me tonight during the second watch.'

Nu could hear the man chuckle.

'Give me your robe,' said Nu, 'that all may think that it is you,' and he reached his hand for the horn crowned aurochs skin.

Throk passed it over, only too glad to drop back again into the slumber that his fellow had disturbed. Nu drew the bull's head over his own, the muzzle projecting like a visor, and the whole sitting low upon his head threw his features into shadow. Nu stepped out upon the platform. The other sentry was standing impatiently waiting his coming, at sight of him the fellow turned and walked toward one of the dwellings that stretched further into the lake. There were seven in all that were joined to the shore by this single causeway – Nu had entered the one nearest the land.

In which was the prisoner, and was she even in any of this particular collection of dwellings? It was equally possible that she might be in one of the others of which Nu had counted not less than ten stretching along the shore of the lake for at least a mile or more. But he was sure that they had first brought her to one of the dwellings of this unit – he had seen them cross the causeway with her. Whether they had removed her to some other village later, he could not know. If there was only some way to learn definitely. He thought of the accommodating and sleepy Throk – would he dare venture another assault upon the lunk-head's credulity. Nu shrugged. The chances were more than even that he would not find the girl before dawn without help, and that whether he did or no he never would escape from the village with his life. What was life anyway, but a series of chances, great and small. He had taken chances before – well, he would take this one.

He reentered the dwelling and walked noisily to Throk's side. Stooping he shook the man by the shoulder. Throk opened his eyes.

'In which place is the prisoner?' asked Nu. He had come near to saying cave, but he had heard Gron speak of the hide and thatch things which protected them from the rains by another name than cave, and so he was bright enough to guess that he might betray himself if he used the word here.

For the most part his language and the language of the Lake Dwellers was identical, and so he used a word which meant, roughly, in exactly what spot was the captive secured.

'In the last one, of course,' grumbled the sleepy Throk.

Nu did not dare question him further. The last one might mean the last of this unit of dwellings or it might mean that she was in the last village, and Nu did not know which the last village might be, whether north or south of the village where he was. Already he could feel the eyes of the man searching through the darkness toward him. Nu rose and turned toward the doorway. Had the fellow's suspicions been aroused – had Nu gone too far?

Throk sat upright upon his hides watching the retreating figure – in his dense mind questions were revolving. Who was this man? Of course he must know him, but somehow he could not place his voice. Why had he asked where the captive was imprisoned? Everyone in all the villages knew that well enough. Throk became uneasy. He did not like the looks of things. He started to rise. Ugh! how sleepy he was. What was the use, anyway? It was all right, of course. He lay back again upon his aurochs skins.

Outside Nu walked to the shore and replenished the beast-fire. Then he turned back up the causeway. Quickly he continued along the platforms past the several dwellings until he had come to the last of the seven. At the doorway he paused and listened, at the same time sniffing quietly. A sudden tremor ran through his giant frame, his heart, throbbing wildly, leaped to his throat – Nat-ul was within!

He crossed the threshold – the building was a small one. No other scent of human being had mingled with that of Nat-ul. She must be alone. Nu groped through the darkness, feeling with his hands in the air before him and his sandaled feet upon the floor. His delicate nostrils guided him too, and at last he came upon her, lying tightly bound to an upright at the far end of the room.

He bent low over her. She was asleep. He laid a hand upon her shoulder and as he felt her stir he placed his other palm across her lips and bending his mouth close to her ear whispered that she must make no outcry.

Nat-ul opened her eyes and stirred.

'S-sh,' cautioned Nu. 'It is I, Nu, the son of Nu.' He removed his hand from her lips and raised her to a sitting posture, kneeling at her side. He put his arms about her, a word of endearment on his lips; but she pushed him away.

'What do you here?' she asked, coldly.

Nu was stunned with the surprise of it.

'I have come to save you,' he whispered; 'to take you back to the cliffs beside the Restless Sea, where our people dwell.'

'Go away!' replied Nat-ul. 'Go back to your woman.'

'Nat-ul!' exclaimed Nu. 'What has happened? What has changed you? Has the sickness come upon you, because of what you have endured – the sickness that changes the mind of its victim into the mind of one of the ape-folk? There is no woman for Nu but Nat-ul, the daughter of Tha.'

'There is the stranger woman, Gron,' cried Nat-ul bitterly. 'I saw her in your arms – I saw your lips meet, and then I ran away. Go back to her. I wish to die.'

Nu sought her hand, holding it tight.

'You saw what you saw, Nat-ul,' he said; 'but you did not hear when I told Gron that I loved only you. You did not see me disengage her arms. Then I saw you far away, and the herders come and take you, and I did not even cast another look upon the stranger woman; but hurried after your captors, hiding close by until darkness came. That I am here, Nat-ul, should prove my love, if ever you could have doubted it. Oh, Nat-ul, Nat-ul, how could you doubt the love of Nu!'

The girl read as much in his manner as his words that he spoke the truth, and even had he lied she would surely have believed him, so great was her wish to hear the very words he spoke. She dropped her cheek to his hand with a little sigh of relief and happiness, and then he took her in his arms. But only a moment could they spare to sentiment – stern necessity called upon them for action, immediate and swift. How urgent was the call Nu would have guessed could he have looked into the hut where Throk lay upon his aurochs skins, wide eyed.

The man's muddy brain revolved many times the details

of the coming of the fellow who had just asked the whereabouts of the prisoner. It was all quite strange, and the more that Throk thought upon it the more fully awake he became and the better able to realize that there had been something altogether too unusual and mysterious in the odd request and actions of the stranger.

Throk sat up. He had suddenly realized what would befall him should anything happen to the community because of his neglect of duty – the primitive communal laws were harsh, the results of their infringement, sudden and relentless. He jumped to his feet, all excitement now. Not waiting to find a skin to throw over his shoulders, he grasped his weapons and ran out upon the platform. A quick glance revealed the fact that no sentry was in sight where a sentry should have been. He recalled the stranger's query about the location of the captive, and turned his face in the direction of the further dwellings.

Running swiftly and silently he hastened toward the hut in which Nat-ul had been confined, and so it was that as Nu emerged he found a naked warrior almost upon him. At sight of Nu and the girl behind him Throk raised his voice in a loud cry of alarm. His spear hand flew back, but back, too, flew the spear hand of Nu, the son of Nu. Two weapons flew simultaneously, and at the same instant Nat-ul, Nu and Throk dropped to the planking to avoid the missiles. Both whizzed harmlessly above them, and then the two warriors rushed upon one another with upraised axes.

From every doorway men were pouring in response to Throk's cry. Nu could not wait to close with his antagonist. He must risk the loss of the encounter and his ax as well in one swift move. Behind his shoulder his ax hand paused for an instant, then shot forward and released the heavy weapon. With the force of a cannon ball the crude stone implement flew through the air, striking Throk full in the face, crushing his countenance to a mangled blur of bloody flesh.

As the Lake Dweller stumbled forward dead, Nu grasped Nat-ul's hand and dragged her around the corner of the dwelling out of sight of the advancing warriors who were dashing toward them with savage shouts and menacing weapons. At the rail of the platform Nu seized Nat-ul and lifted her over, dropping her into the water beneath as he vaulted over at her side.

A few strong strokes carried them well under the village, and as they forged toward the shore they could hear the searchers running hither and thither above them. The whole community was awake by now, and the din was deafening. As the two crawled from the water to the shore they were instantly discovered by those nearest them, and at once the causeway rattled and groaned beneath the feet of a hundred warriors that sped along it to intercept the flight of the fugitives.

Ahead of them were the dangers of the primeval night; behind them were no less grave dangers at the hands of their savage foes. Unarmed, but for a knife, it was futile to stand and fight. The only hope lay in flight and the chance that they might reach the forest and a sheltering tree before either the human beasts behind them or the beasts of prey before had seized them.

Both Nu and Nat-ul were fleet of foot. Beside them, the Lake Dwellers were sluggards, and consequently five minutes put them far ahead of their pursuers, who, seeing the futility of further pursuit and the danger of being led too far from their dwellings and possibly into a strong camp of enemies, abandoned the chase and returned to the lake.

Fortune favored Nu and Nat-ul, as it is ever credited with favoring the brave. They reached the forest at the edge of the plateau without encountering any of the more formidable carnivora. Here they found sanctuary in a tree where they remained until dawn. Then they resumed their way toward the cliffs which they must scale to reach the sea. The matter of Gron had been settled between them – they would offer to take her with them back to their own people where she might live in safety so long as she chose.

It was daylight when Nu and Nat-ul reached the base of the cliffs. Gron was not in sight. At the summit of the cliff, however, two crafty eyes looked from behind a grassy screen upon them. The watcher saw the man and the maid, and recognized them both. They were ascending – he would wait a bit.

Nu and Nat-ul climbed easily upward. When they had gained about half the distance toward the summit the man, shunning further concealment, started downward to meet them. His awkwardness started a loose stone and appraised them of his presence. Nu looked up, as did Nat-ul.

'Tur!' exclaimed the latter.

'Tur,' echoed Nu, and redoubled his efforts to ascend.

'You are unarmed,' cautioned Nat-ul, 'and he is above. The advantage is all his.'

But the cave man was hot to lay hands upon this fellow who had brought upon Nat-ul all the hardships she had suffered. He loosed his knife and carried it between his teeth, ready for instant use. Like a cat he scrambled up the steep ascent. Directly at his heels came his sweet and savage Nat-ul. Between her strong, white teeth was her own knife. Tur was in for a warm reception. He had reached a ledge now just below a cave mouth. Lying loosely upon the cliff-side, scarcely balanced there, was a huge rock, a ton or two of potential destruction. Tur espied it. Just below it, directly in its path, climbed Nu and Nat-ul. Tur grasped in an instant the possibilities that lay in the mighty weight of that huge boulder. He leaped behind it, and bracing his feet against it and his back against the cliff, pushed. The boulder leaned and rocked. Nu, realizing the danger, looked to right and left for an avenue of escape, but chance had played well into the hands of the enemy. Just at this point there was no foothold other than directly where they stood. They redoubled their efforts to reach the man before he could dislodge the boulder.

Tur redoubled his efforts to start it spinning down upon them. He changed his position, placing his shoulder against the rock and one hand and foot against the cliff. Thus he pushed frantically. The hideous menace to those below it swayed and rocked. Another moment and it would topple downward.

Presently from the cave behind Tur a woman emerged, awakened by the noises from without. It was Gron. She took in the whole scene in a single glance. She saw Nu and with him Nat-ul. The man she loved with the woman who stood between them, who must always stand between them, for she realized that Nu would never love her, whether Nat-ul were alive or dead.

She smiled as she saw success about to crown the efforts of Tur. In another instant the man who scorned her love and the woman she hated with all the power of her savage jealousy would be hurled, crushed and mangled, to the bottom of the cliff.

Tur! She watched her mate with suddenly narrowing eyes. Tur! He struck her! He repudiated her! A flush of shame scorched her cheek. Tur! Her mate. The father of her child!

The rock toppled. Nu and Nat-ul from below were clambering upward. The man had seen Gron, but he had read her emotions clearly. No use to call upon her for help. Out of the past the old love for her true mate had sprung to claim her. She would cleave to Tur in the moment of his victory, hoping thus to win him back. Nor was Nu insensible to the power of hatred which he might have engendered in the woman's breast by repulsing her demonstrations of love.

Another push like the last and the boulder would lunge down upon them. Gron stood with her hands clutching her naked breasts, the nails buried in the soft flesh until blood trickled down the bronze skin. The father of her child. Her child! The pitiful thing that she deserted within the shelter by the beach! Her baby – her dead baby! Dead because of Tur and his cruelty toward her.

Tur braced himself for the final push. A smile curled his lip. His back was toward Gron – otherwise he would not have smiled. Even Nu did not smile at the thing he saw above him – the face of a woman made hideous by hate and blood-lust. With bared knife Gron leaped toward Tur. The upraised knife buried itself in his back and chest. With a scream he turned toward the avenger. As his eyes rested upon the face of the mother of his child, he shrieked aloud, and with the shriek still upon his lips he sank to the ledge, dead.

Then Gron turned to face the two who were rapidly ascending toward her. Words of thanks were already upon Nu's lips; but Gron stood silent, ready to meet them – with bared knife. What would she do? Nu and Nat-ul wondered, but there was no retreat and only a knife-armed woman barred their way to liberty and home.

Nu was almost level with her. Gron raised her knife above her head. Nu sprang upward to strike the weapon to one side before it was buried in his breast; but Gron was too quick for him. The blade fell, but not upon Nu. Deep into her own broken heart Gron plunged the sharp point, and at the same instant she leaped far beyond Nu and Nat-ul to crash, mangled and broken at the foot of the lofty cliff.

Death, sudden and horrible, was no stranger to these primeval lovers. They saw that Gron was dead, and Tur, likewise. Nu appropriated the latter's weapons, and side by side the two set out to find the beach. They found it with only such delays and dangers as were daily incidents in their savage lives. They found the boat, too, and reached the mainland and, later, the cliffs and their tribe, in safety. Here they found a wild welcome awaiting them, for both had been given up as dead.

That night they walked hand in hand beneath the great equatorial moon, beside the Restless Sea.

'Soon,' said Nu, 'Nat-ul shall become the mate of Nu, the son of Nu. Nu, my father, hath said it, and so, too, had spoken Tha, the father of Nat-ul. At the birth of the next moon we are to mate.'

Nat-ul nestled closer to him.

'My Nu is a great warrior,' she said, 'and a great hunter, but he has not brought back the head of Oo, the killer of men and mammoths, that he promised to lay before the cave of Tha, my father.'

'Nu sets out at the breaking of the next light to hunt Oo,' he answered quietly, 'nor will he return to claim his mate until he has taken the head of the killer of men and mammoths.'

Nat-ul laughed up into Nu's face.

'Nat-ul but joked,' she said. 'My man has proved himself

greater than a hunter of Oo. I do not want the great othed head, Nu. I only want you. You must not go forth hunt the beast – it is enough that you could slay him were e to attack us, and none there is who dares say it be b nd you.'

'Nevertheless I hunt Oo on the morrow,' insisted N have never forgotten my promise.'

Nat-ul tried to dissuade him, but he was obdurate, an next morning Nu, the son of Nu, set forth from the beside the Restless Sea to hunt the lair of Oo.

All day Nat-ul sat waiting his return though she knew it might be days before he came back, or that he migh come at all. Grave premonitions of impending da haunted her. She wandered in and out of her cave, loo for the thousandth time along the way that Nu might cc

Suddenly a rumbling rose from far inland. The e shook and trembled. Nat-ul, wide eyed with terror, saw people fleeing upward toward their caves. The hea became overcast, the loud rumbling rose to a hideous deafening roar. The violence of the earth's motion increas until the very cliffs in which the people hid rocked ar shook like a leaf before a hurricane.

Nat-ul ran to the innermost recess of her father's cave. There she huddled upon the floor burying her face in a pile of bear and lion skins. About her clustered other members of her father's family – all were terror stricken.

It was five minutes before the end came. It came in one awful hideous convulsion that lifted the mighty cliff a hundred feet aloft, cracking and shattering it to fragments as its face toppled forward into the forest at its foot. Then there was silence – silence awful and ominous. For five minutes the quiet of death reigned upon the face of the earth, until presently from far out at sea came a rushing, swirling sound – a sound that only a few wild beasts were left to hear – and the ocean, mountain high, rushed in upon what had been the village of Nu, the chief.

CHAPTER FIFTEEN

WHAT THE CAVE REVEALED

hen Victoria Custer opened her eyes the first face that she w was that of her brother, Barney, bent above her. She oked at him in puzzled bewilderment for a moment. Presntly she reached her hands toward him.

'Where am I?' she asked. 'What has happened?'

'You're all right, Vic,' replied the young man. 'You're safe nd sound in Lord Greystoke's bungalow.'

For another moment the girl knit her brows in perplexity.

'But the earthquake,' she asked, 'wasn't there an earthquake?'

'A little one, Vic, but it didn't amount to anything – there wasn't any damage done.'

'How long have I been – er – this way?' she continued.

'You swooned about three minutes ago,' replied her brother. 'I just put you down here and sent Esmeralda for some brandy when you opened your eyes.'

'Three minutes,' murmured the girl – 'three minutes!'

That night after the others had retired Barney Custer sat beside his sister's bed, and long into the early morning she told him in simple words and without sign of hysteria the story that I have told here, of Nat-ul and Nu, the son of Nu.

'I think,' she said, when she had finished the strange tale, 'that I shall be happier for this vision, or whatever one may call it. I have met my dream man and lived again the life that he and I lived countless ages ago. Even if he comes to me in my dreams again it will not disturb me. I am glad that it was but a dream, and that Mr Curtiss was not killed by Terkoz, and that all those other terrible things were not real.'

'Now,' said Barney, with a smile, 'you may be able to listen to what Curtiss has been trying to tell you.' It was a half question.

Victoria Custer shook her head.

'No,' she said, 'I could never love him now. I cannot tell you why, but it may be that what I have lived through in those three minutes revealed more than the dim and distant past. Terkoz has never liked him, you know.'

Barney did not pursue the subject. He kissed the girl good night and as the east commenced to lighten to the coming dawn he sought his own room and a few hours' sleep.

The next day it was decided that Victoria and Barney should start for the coast as soon as porters could be procured, which would require but a few days at the most. Lieutenant Butzow, Curtiss and I decided to accompany them.

It was the last day of their stay at the Greystoke ranch. The others were hunting. Barney and Victoria had remained to put the finishing touches upon their packing, but that was done now and the girl begged for a last ride over the broad, game dotted valley of Uziri.

Before they had covered a mile Barney saw that his sister had some particular objective in mind, for she rode straight as an arrow and rapidly, with scarce a word, straight south toward the foot of the rugged mountains that bound the Waziri's country upon that side – in the very direction that she had previously shunned. After a couple of hours of stiff riding they came to the foot of the lofty cliff that had formerly so filled Victoria with terror and misgivings.

'What's the idea, Vic,' asked the man, 'I thought you were through with all this.'

'I am, Barney,' she replied, 'or will be after today, but I just couldn't go away without satisfying my curiosity. I want to know that there is no cave here in which a man might be buried.

She dismounted and started to climb the rugged escarpment. Barney was amazed at the agility and strength of the slender girl. It kept him puffing to remain near her in her rapid ascent.

At last she stopped suddenly upon a narrow ledge. When

Barney reached her side he saw that she was very white, and he paled himself when he saw what her eyes rested upon. The earthquake had dislodged a great boulder that for ages evidently had formed a part of the face of the cliff. Now it had tilted outward a half dozen feet, revealing behind it the mouth of a gloomy cavern.

Barney took Victoria's hand. It was very cold and trembled a little.

'Come,' he said, 'this has gone far enough, Vic. You'll be sick again if you keep it up. Come back to the horses – we've seen all we want to see.'

She shook her head.

'Not until I have searched that cave,' she said, almost defiantly, and Barney knew that she would have her way.

Together they entered the forbidding grotto, Barney in advance, striking matches with one hand while he clung to his cocked rifle with the other; but there was nothing there that longer had the power to injure.

In a far corner the feeble rays of the match lighted something that brought Barney to a sudden halt. He tried to turn the girl back as though there was nothing more to be seen, but she had seen too and pressed forward. She made her brother light another match, and there before them lay the crumbling skeleton of a large man. By its side rested a broken, stone-tipped spear, and there was a stone knife and a stone ax as well.

'Look!' whispered the girl, pointing to something that lay just beyond the skeleton.

Barney raised the match he held until its feeble flame carried to that other object – the grinning skull of a great cat, its upper jaw armed with two mighty, eighteen-inch, curved fangs.

'Oo, the killer of men and of mammals,' whispered Victoria Custer, in an awed voice, 'and Nu, the son of Nu, who killed him for his Nat-ul – for me!'

THE END

COSMOLOGY (NF)

STAR

	Adi-Kent Thomas Jeffrey	
0352398280	**THE BERMUDA TRIANGLE**	50p
0352398620	**THEY DARED THE DEVIL'S TRIANGLE**	50p
	Jack Stoneley & A. T. Lawton	
0352300604	**IS ANYONE OUT THERE?**	55p

TANDEM

	P. Moore & I. Nicholson	
0426088387	**BLACK HOLES IN SPACE**	40p
	Elizabeth Nichols	
0426162994	**THE DEVIL'S SEA**	40p
	Ivan T. Sanderson	
0426138805	**INVISIBLE RESIDENTS**	40p
0426138724	**UNINVITED VISITORS**	40p
	Arthur Shuttlewood	
0426169263	**THE WARMINSTER MYSTERY**	50p
	Brad Steiger and Joan Whritenour	
0426163281	**FLYING SAUCERS ARE HOSTILE**	40p
0426134427	**THE NEW U.F.O. BREAKTHROUGH**	35p
0426163362	**STRANGERS FROM THE SKIES**	40p
	Paul Thomas	
0426127226	**FLYING SAUCERS THROUGH THE AGES**	35p
	B. Le Poer Trench	
0426134508	**OPERATION EARTH**	35p
	Jacques Vallée	
0426130715	**ANATOMY OF A PHENOMENON**	35p
0426157397	**PASSPORT TO MAGONIA**	45p

GAMES & PASTIMES (NF)

STAR

0352300027	Prince Obolensky **BACKGAMMON**	90p
0352398124	Tim Holland **BEGINNING BACKGAMMON**	95p
0352300574	Joe Davis **HOW I PLAY SNOOKER** (illus)	80p
0352300493	Richard L. Frey **HOW TO WIN AT CONTRACT BRIDGE**	85p
0352300132	Terence Reese **PRECISION BIDDING AND PRECISION PLAY**	50p

TANDEM

0426159142	Lelia Hattersley **BACKGAMMON TO WIN**	40p
042612829X	L. G. Horsefield **CROSS-FIGURE PUZZLES NO. 2**	25p
0426149718	**CROSS-FIGURE PUZZLES NO. 3**	30p
0426172248	**CROSS-FIGURE PUZZLES NO. 4**	50p
0426139011	**CODEWORDS**	35p
0426149637	**CODEWORDS NO. 2**	35p
0426169425	**CODEWORDS NO. 3**	45p
0426169778	**FILL IN PUZZLES NO. 1**	45p
0426169697	Jean Andrew (editor) **HIDDEN NUMBERS 1**	45p
0426169506	**HIDDEN WORDS NO. 1**	45p
0426172329	**HIDDEN WORDS NO. 2**	45p
0426145682	A. H. Thrower **NEW GUIDE TO I.Q. TESTS**	35p
0426164083	Norman Sullivan **SULLIVAN'S I.Q. TESTS**	50p

Fantasy Fiction

John Norman

Tarl Cabot's adventures in the fabulous Counter-Earth of Gor

Tarnsman of Gor	60p
Outlaw of Gor	70p
Priest-Kings of Gor	50p
Nomads of Gor	45p
Assassins of Gor	45p
Raiders of Gor	40p
Captive of Gor	60p
Hunters of Gor	45p
Marauders of Gor	60p

John Jakes

The exploits of Brak the Barbarian

Brak the Barbarian	45p
The Sorceress	45p
The Mark of the Demon	45p

Jane Gaskell

Sorcery and the clash of arms in the pre-dawn of forgotten worlds

The Serpent	60p
The Dragon	45p
Atlan	60p
The City	45p

Name ....

Address ....

Titles required ....

....

....

....

....

....

....